THE FOOLISH

FRIEND

ELIZABETH

BRAMWELL

chinook
sun

All the characters and scenes in this book are a
work of fiction, unfortunately, because I really
wish the Shropshires and the Devenishes had been
real. Any similarity to real people, living or dead,
is purely coincidental.

ISBN: 978-1-9994096-3-0

DEDICATION

For Katie

Because we all need a best friend willing to laugh at
our stupidity while helping us clear up our messes

Also by Elizabeth Bramwell

The Dashing Widow

His Darling Belle

The Rebel Wife

A Novel Miss

His Alter Ego

CHAPTER ONE

James Douglas, 4th Baron of Cottingham, smiled from the doorway of his lifelong friend's front parlour. He'd been able to convince the Marquis of Shropshire's butler - who had known him since he'd still worn leading-strings - that it would be a great joke for him to enter the room unannounced, and be able to surprise both Lady Shropshire and her granddaughter, Lady Henrietta.

So far, it seemed like it had been a good plan. It was early in the Season, but already the Shropshire's afternoon callers numbered in the low teens. Lady Henrietta (although he struggled to think of her as anything but a feisty eight-year-old demanding to be called Henry) sat with a few other young ladies beside the window, their heads together as they giggled over something secretive.

Her grandmother, the redoubtable Marchioness

of Shropshire, held court towards the centre of the room, where half a dozen matrons of the Ton and a smattering of bored-looking young men drank tea and made polite small talk. No doubt the poor gentlemen would be happier chasing after some of the attractive misses sat at the window, but manners demanded they visit with Lady Shropshire rather than her granddaughter's friends.

He walked into the room quietly and without fuss, intending to take a chair beside the Marchioness and see how long it would take for her to notice his presence, when Henry chose that moment to glance in his direction, and then managed to quite ruin his little trick.

"James!" she cried out, jumping to her feet. "I didn't hear you announced!"

He gave her a rueful smile as everyone turned to look at him. "You haven't changed a bit in the last year, Henry, and still manage to ruin a good joke when you have the opportunity."

A couple of the gentlemen laughed, and Henry blushed deeply. As she sank down to her seat, he wondered if he'd hurt her feelings, but before he could reassure her that he'd only been teasing, his attention was claimed by the Marchioness.

"Cottingham, my dear boy, when did you return?" she said, extending her thin hand towards him as he approached. "Your mother must be so happy to have you back in the fold."

"I think she's just relieved that I came back in one piece," he said as he bowed over the older Lady's hand. "As much as I loved Montreal, I confess that it is good to be home."

"We are glad to have your company once again, my boy. It was quite selfish of you to leave us for an entire year; even Henrietta pined for your escort around Hyde Park, didn't you, my love?"

Henry, whose cheeks were still flushed, gave a weak smile in his direction. "Who doesn't like to spend time with their friends?"

Several of the young women were studying him with open curiosity, and he wondered if he had danced with any of them before his departure. He smiled and nodded in their direction, just in case.

"You are all acquainted with Lord Cottingham, I believe?" said Lady Shropshire, gesturing at the entire room with one hand. "He's been in Canada or some such place for the last year, but I've known the boy since he was still in the cradle. His lands march alongside those of Shropshire House, of course, and we've missed him like he was one of the family."

There were a few murmured welcomes, and many bows exchanged, but Lady Shropshire's guests took her hint and began to leave. Henry kissed the last of her friends on the cheek, and only the three of them remained.

"You didn't have to cut short your gathering on my account," said James as he settled himself into a chair.

"Nonsense, I was practically bored to tears by their inane conversation," said Lady Shropshire. "It's too early in the Season for any real gossip to have begun, so most of them are more interested in learning what they can about my great-nephew, Gloucester."

James glanced at Henry for an explanation, but she raised her brows in surprise.

"I told you in my letters, James. Cousin Gloucester ran off and married a trade widow called Abby near the end of last Season in a havey-cavey manner."

"Ah, I remember now," he said, but Henry narrowed her gaze at him.

"You never read that letter, did you?"

He felt his cheeks warm a little and resisted the urge to tug at his cravat. "I'm sorry, Henry; I was dashed busy while in Montreal learning all about the estate's investments in the Hudson Bay Company, not to mention getting my brother settled into his new role out there. I'm afraid that I didn't have the leisure to read."

"And on the ship back?" she asked, something between anger and hurt dancing in her eyes. "I suppose in all those endless hours in your cabin, you were too busy as well."

"Hush my dear," admonished her grandmother. "Gentlemen have a quite surprising amount of work they need to accomplish in any given day, and no doubt he would have read your letters if he'd had the time. Isn't that so, Cottingham?"

The sharp look resting on Lady Shropshire's face suggested that she didn't mean a word of what she'd said, causing his cheeks to heat further.

"Yes, of course, although I'm dashed sorry for it, Henry. I'll read them as soon as I'm home, how's that?"

The smile Henry flashed was a sickly one, and James had the uncomfortable feeling that he'd hurt her feelings once again.

"No need for that now, as I'm sure you'll be twice as busy in London as you were in Montreal. Besides, you're here now, so I suppose I can just tell you everything you need to know about what you missed, including my cousin's marriage."

"I would like that," he said, and was relieved to see Lady Shropshire give a small nod of approval.

"Not that there was any reason for Gloucester to run off the way he did," sniffed the Marchioness.

"He's made it harder for his new wife to be accepted by the Ton, of course, but the family is determined to support the new Countess of Gloucester - and anyone who chooses not to accept her shall incur my censure!"

"And that's not something anyone would dare risk," said James, only half joking. The Marchioness of Shropshire may have been in her early seventies, but the Ton still looked to her for guidance on such matters.

"I don't think it will take long for Abby to win them all over anyway," said Henry. "She hasn't been in any sort of scrapes since they got married - at least, none that are of consequence! Besides, she makes Cousin Gloucester smile, and anyone who can do that will be able to bring the Ton to heel."

"I take it you like her, then?" asked James, and Henry turned her large brown eyes onto him.

"Very much, as I explained in my letters. The entire family descended on Gloucester House over Christmas, and she utterly charmed us all as the perfect hostess. Why, Grandpapa is still talking about the food that was served, and complains that our cook just cannot roast duck to the same high standard."

"Which reminds me, I must go and speak with the cook about ordering some desserts from Gunters for our dinner party tomorrow," said the Marchioness as she got to her feet. "No, there's no need to leave on my account, Cottingham. You're practically family so I'm sure there can be no censure in you talking with Henrietta for another ten minutes – you can beg her leave to dance with you at the Loughcroft's ball this evening."

"I'm afraid I didn't receive an invitation," said James, not that he wanted one anyway. He was a wealthy bachelor in his mid-twenties, which meant that every ball he attended inevitably descended into a game of dodge-the-matchmakers who all seemed determined to shackle him to some dull, worthy girl who would bore him to tears within minutes.

"Nonsense my boy; your mother was invited, and naturally that extends to you as well. I shall inform Emma at dinner this evening that she is to expect you, and also arrange for a private supper next week so that you can regale us all with tales of Montreal."

The Marchioness clicked the library door shut behind her, and Henry shook her head in apparent amusement of the impropriety of the situation.

"For all the world as though we are still muddy children, and not of marriageable age!"

James smiled, glad that she could see the absurdity of the situation as well. "Should I remain in the hope that your Grandfather does not walk in the room and demand that I do the honourable thing?"

She glanced down at her hands. "Oh, I could do much worse than marrying you, I suppose. At least you aren't going to start writing sonnets that compare my left earlobe to a tulip, or some such idiotic nonsense."

"You don't mean to tell me that some poor sop is so in love with you that he's resorted to poetry?"

For a moment, it looked as though she was irritated by his comment, but the serene smile returned so quickly that James supposed he had imagined it.

"It's far worse than that, you know. I took pity on Herbert Filey a few weeks ago, because he's not very confident around ladies and the others can make dreadful fun of him. They started to mock his poetry when they learned he had dedicated some particularly awful verses to me, so I said I found them very pretty."

"And now?" he asked, a smile twitching on the corner of his lips.

She sighed. "Now they are all trying to outdo themselves by writing odes in my honour about everything from my grace and deportment to my perfect fingernails, and each one is worse than the last."

He let loose his laughter, unable to stop himself from remembering a younger version of Henry refusing to memorise Shakespeare's sonnets, and instead declaring the Bard to be a prosy old bore.

"It isn't funny, you know. I know they all think it's a great joke, but it's a sad trial to me," she said, although she was smiling.

"My apologies, Henry. I had no idea of the problems a beautiful heiress must endure."

Her smile faltered, and although she didn't quite scowl, she looked decidedly mulish. "Don't be such a bore, James. You wouldn't find it much fun if your inamoratas all started writing poems about the shape of your nostrils, now would you?"

The image was a striking one, and James couldn't help but shudder at the thought. "Good God, no, but for a start, I do not have any inamoratas – and how the devil do you know anything about them, anyway?"

Henry waved a hand at nothing in particular. "Grandpapa was concerned you were running away to Canada with an opera dancer – and no, I have no idea where he picked up such a notion."

It took James a moment to collect himself before he could actually speak. "I don't think that you should speak so freely of such things in front of gentlemen, Henry."

She turned those wide eyes onto him again. "I can hardly influence what subjects Grandpapa chooses to discuss with me, James, but you are of course free to explain to him what are appropriate topics of conversation for him to share with his granddaughter."

James opened and closed his mouth a few times as a witty comeback refused to present itself, so he settled on a rueful smile instead. "Wretch! You don't change, do you?"

"On the contrary, I have it on good authority that I've changed a great deal in the last year."

James nodded. "Acquired some town bronze. Don't worry about that, Henry; I promise that you'll always be a hoydenish eight-year-old to my mud-splattered, twelve-year-old self."

"How reassuring," she replied, and he got the feeling that her smile didn't go more than skin deep.

In truth, she had changed since their carefree childhood spent romping across their respective estates and getting themselves into all manner of trouble. They'd been thick as thieves as children, for a mutual love of the outdoors and playing pranks had inevitably brought them together.

Then he'd been sent away to Eton, and she'd been schooled in the ways of being a Lady. She'd grown into pretty enough girl in her last three seasons, always dressed in modest white gowns and with her hair smoothed back to a bun at the nape of her neck. If there were times when he felt that her demure behaviour bordered on the insipid, he reminded himself that she was only adopting the fashionable air looked on approvingly by more established members of the Ton, and complimented her accordingly.

"Did you really not read my letters?" she blurted out without warning.

James sighed, and tugged once again at his cravat. He'd read each letter with pleasure as he'd received them, but for the life of him, he couldn't recall a single word that she'd written. He'd consumed them as though she was there beside him, telling him all of the gossip he'd missed, before he'd put them away and forgotten their contents in the day-to-day life of Montreal.

Somehow, he doubted she would be any more flattered by the truth than by her assumption that he'd never so much as broken the seal. If he'd had any sense at all he would have read them on the ship on his way back from Canada to remind him of what she'd said, but he'd been sick as a dog for most of the voyage, and that was not something he wished to share with her, either.

"I'm sorry, Henry, but with my younger brother to set up and the investments to review, I suppose I simply forgot about them."

Her smile was tight. "No need to apologise

again, James. It seems reasonable enough to expect you would be bored to tears by letters about my life."

"Never," he declared. "I'm desperate to learn everything that you've been up to while I've been gone."

"Nothing that you don't already know, I suppose. I am entering my fourth Season, and the tabbies are beginning to sharpen their claws. It is a great delight of theirs that even an heiress such as myself can reach twenty-one and still be unwed."

"But how is this?" asked James. "You've told me yourself that half of the Ton is writing poetry celebrating the length of your eyelashes. Surely one or two of them have come up to scratch?"

"Four, actually."

"You're joking!" he found himself sputtering.

"Not in the least," replied Henry, the demure way she folded her hands into her lap defying the steel in her voice. "Two were gazetted fortune hunters, to be sure, but the others would not have been contemptible matches."

"Then why on earth would you not accept one of them?"

She gave a surprising elegant shrug, but looked over her shoulder and out of the window as she replied. "Because I want something more than that."

"Hanging out for a coronet, are you? A laudable enough goal, I suppose, but I hope our friendship allows for me to be blunt and say that after four seasons, it is unlikely for you to make a brilliant match."

She made a sound that could have been a laugh, or quite possibly a sob. "Very true, I daresay. However, I'm not holding out for a brilliant match, as I would very much like to marry for love."

James shook his head at the discovery that the mud-covered urchin of his youth had apparently gained a world view more suited to romantic novels. "I always thought you were smarter than that."

She turned to face him with a frown. "In what way?"

"That you were too intelligent to be swayed by this silly fashion for True Love and all that rot. I know you've somehow got it into your head that love will sweep you off your feet and be a grand adventure, but it doesn't happen that way for most people."

"It worked for my cousins; Emma married Loughcroft, and Gloucester just married Abby not eight months ago," she replied, looking mulish again.

James sighed. "They were the exception, and you know it. You said it yourself: you've been out for four seasons. Surely if you were going to fall head over heels in love with a worthy swain then it would have happened by this point. Marrying a good, kind gentleman for whom you feel affection is a much more realistic proposition."

Henry studied him for a moment, and he had the uncomfortable feeling that she was seeing him with new eyes – and that neither of them would like what she found. "Is that all you want from a marriage, James? Kindness and affection?"

A strange sensation churned in his gut, although he had no words to describe it. "Isn't that what everyone wants?"

"No, some of us want more than that," she said with a sigh. "Besides, you are wrong about me. I am very much head over heels in love with a worthy gentleman."

James started at this revelation. "Good God, since when? And why haven't you told me before?"

"Because I've been hopelessly in love with him for an age," she replied, which for Henry could mean anything from five minutes to five months. "However, he has not shown the slightest inclination to court me despite much encouragement, so there's little point in hope."

Without thinking, James moved to his knees beside Henry's chair in order to capture her hand.

"Then the man you love is a fool who doesn't deserve you," he said softly, genuinely saddened that any man could think to break the heart of his lifelong friend.

Henry laughed, and the sound was bitter enough to remind him that she was more grown-up than he sometimes remembered.

"I've told myself that often enough," she said. She stared forlornly into the fireplace for a moment before giving herself a little shake. "Well, congratulations, James, you've managed to accomplish something Grandmama never has."

He frowned at her. "What would that be?"

"Convinced me that I need to throw myself into this business of catching a husband."

James stood, knowing Henry too well to be surprised at her sudden change of heart, but disliking it all the same. "I never said you needed to throw yourself into it, precisely."

Henry held up a hand to silence him. "No, there is no need to harangue me further; I will consult with Grandmama and do my very best to be open to accepting the suit of some – how did you put it? – some kind gentleman that I can hold in mutual affection."

She clambered up to her feet with all the grace of a bear cub before smoothing the creases out of her dress. She did not look at him directly, and for the life of him, James couldn't quite place the emotions that were dancing all across her face.

"You look like you are preparing yourself to face the gallows," he said, trying to joke with her. She lifted her large brown eyes to his once again, and for some unknown reason, he felt his heart skip a beat.

"No, just the parson's mousetrap. I can count on your help during my search, though, can I not?"

"My help?"

"Yes, in choosing a suitable husband. After all, you know me better than anyone save my grandparents – and Lord knows that they have betrayed some terrible judgement on this matter. Grandpapa insists on keeping copies of the poetry, and swears he will grant his blessing to whoever comes up with the most entertaining verse."

"I-" for some unknown reason, words failed James completely as she stared at him with the type of trust that can only be formed over a lifetime of friendship. "I don't know how much use I would be."

She smiled. "I think you will prove extremely useful – and you can begin by thinking about which gentlemen of your acquaintance are seeking marriage. I don't mind if the man in question is poor so long as he has birth and looks to recommend him, but no fortune hunters – somehow I doubt they will remain kind and affectionate once my dowry is placed into their hands. Now, I will have to shoo you out so that I can go and tell Grandmama that I am willing and ready to get myself leg-shackled."

James found himself being unceremoniously hurried out to the hallway, where the Shropshire's butler was already waiting for him with his hat and gloves. "I say, Henry, this is starting to sound awfully like one of your queer starts."

"Nonsense, husband-hunting is a perfectly acceptable pastime for a woman of my age and rank," she told him with a dazzling smile. "And who better to help me out than my childhood best friend? If we rub along together famously, then surely I could find affection with one of your male friends as well?"

None that he would not have to call out immediately afterwards, James told himself – and was then surprised at the violence of his own thoughts.

"I suppose-"

"Excellent! You may have the supper dance with me at the Loughcroft's ball tonight – you know Grandmama will never forgive you if you don't go, don't you? – and then during supper, you can let me know who you think might make me a good husband," said Henry, her eyes bright for some reason he could not explain.

James wanted to say something to reassure her, for he was observant enough to know that she was upset and worried that his well-intentioned words had upset her, but before he knew precisely what had happened he found himself on the front steps of the Shropshire's Mayfair home as the butler firmly – but respectfully – closed the door in his face.

"Help Henry find a husband?" he said to himself with a faint trace of disgust. For some reason, he could not find any enthusiasm for the task at all.

CHAPTER TWO

Of all the irritatingly blockheaded, idiotic, self-centred males Henrietta had met during her lifetime – and there were many – James Douglas was undoubtedly the most annoying, the most selfish, and the most unashamedly blockheaded out of them all.

It took every last iota of self-restraint to prevent Henrietta from stomping up the staircase to her room and from giving the door a satisfying slam shut behind her. She paced about for a good two minutes in a futile bid to calm herself, before flinging herself down onto her large bed.

"Why are men so stupid?" she screamed into the blankets, trusting the noise would be muted enough by the goose-down to prevent her maid from running in to tend her. "I hate you, James Douglas. I hate you. I hate you. I hate you."

It didn't help. No matter how much she tried to stoke the flames of her anger, it died before it could catch and was replaced by a fit of the blue devils.

There was no point in denying it. She loved James and had since she was 8 years old, when he'd untangled a caterpillar from her unruly blonde curls. It was possible she'd loved him before that as well, but the moment he had smiled at her and promised that the wriggly worm was not going to hurt her, she'd been lost to James Douglas and convinced that one day she would be his wife.

Unfortunately, James appeared oblivious to the fact that they were fated to be together, and quite possibly still believed she was a grubby little girl forever getting bugs tangled up in her hair.

"You were supposed to miss me terribly," she muttered into the blankets. "I'd have never encouraged you to go otherwise, you stupid fool."

There was a knock at her door, and before she had a chance to respond, it opened to reveal her grandparents. Henrietta scrambled up off the bed as they stepped into the room.

"Henrietta darling, are you quite well?" asked her Grandmama as she entered the room, her Grandpapa not five paces behind.

"We heard you trying your very best not to be

overheard as you screamed," explained the Marquis, his voice still stronger than that of a man in his prime, despite the fact he'd celebrated his eighty-fifth birthday only a month earlier.

Henrietta didn't know what to say, or how to explain the churning emotions in her gut that were threatening to make her vomit. Instead, she reached out with both hands and pushed herself into her grandmother's embrace. The Marchioness – not one for physical displays of affection despite her deep love for her family – hesitated for only a moment before wrapping her thin arms tight around Henrietta.

"I'm so sorry I didn't listen to you," sniffed Henrietta, her eyes unaccountably damp. "I don't mean to be such a trial, truly, I don't."

She felt her grandmother relax about her. "Hush you foolish girl, I have no idea what has upset you so much, but there's no need to worry. I'm sure it will all come about."

"But it won't!" Henrietta wailed, no longer caring whether or not she sounded like a petulant child. "Grandmama he didn't even miss me at all!"

The tears came suddenly, and she began to sob into her Grandmama's expensive Chantilly lace gown. Within moments she felt her grandfather's arms about her also, and it seemed like a lifetime's worth of unspent tears flowed down her cheeks as they eased her gently down to sit on the bed, their embrace a cocoon to keep all the world away.

After what felt like forever – but was in truth perhaps five minutes – the tears began to fade, only to be replaced by a stuffed nose, tired eyes, and the hiccups. She sat up as her grandparents released her from their embrace, and accepted the two proffered handkerchiefs with a quiet "thank you".

Her Grandpapa placed a finger beneath her chin and gently eased her to look up at him. He grimaced.

"Promise me you'll never cry in front of a gentleman," said Grandpapa in a despairing voice, which surprised a laugh out of her before she could help it.

"Do I look a complete fright?" she asked, wiping the last traitorous tears away from her eyes.

"Not a complete one, but you made a very valiant attempt at it," said the Marquis with an encouraging smile. She stuck out her tongue, which only made him laugh.

"My poor Henrietta, what happened downstairs? I was only gone for ten minutes," said Grandmama, her thin face a picture of concern.

"It was just something that James said to me, and I've been thinking about it ever since."

"And what was that, my darling?"

She would not cry again.

"That it was high time that I took this marriage business seriously and should consider applying myself to finding a husband," she said, trying to sound unconcerned about his advice, but even she could hear the quiver in her voice.

"I see," said Grandmama, and Henrietta was grateful that the Marchioness did not put her observations into words.

"I suppose he has a point. I don't regret turning down the proposals of those suitors because I am quite certain that I would have made a miserable wife for all of them, but perhaps…"

"Yes, my love?" prompted Grandpapa gently when she couldn't bring herself to finish the thought.

Henrietta took a deep breath and rushed her fence. "Perhaps I have not been as serious as I should have been in looking to make a suitable match."

She felt rather than saw them exchange glances over her bowed head.

"Well, I am happy to hear you admit it," said Grandmama, "Especially when you consider what estimable young men have been haunting this house as of late. However, I confess that I'm confused as to this sudden change of heart when not an hour ago, you swore to your friends that you would never marry."

"I said I'd never marry without love," clarified Henrietta, "and it's an important distinction that I remain devoted to. It is just that, well, perhaps I made the mistake of thinking that love would just come about and find me here waiting for it, instead of setting out to locate it for myself."

She kept her attention firmly on her feet, but the prolonged silence told her that her grandparents were continuing an unspoken conversation over her head. She wondered if they even realised how much she admired and envied them their companionship, or if they took it for granted. They had been married as virtual strangers, but love had grown for them over the years, and they were fond of telling her the tale.

Suddenly they both leant forward, each kissing her on the cheek in a way they hadn't done since she was in leading strings. She gave a mortifyingly childish giggle in response.

"I think that's a splendid idea," announced her Grandpapa with considerable enthusiasm. "You are an intelligent girl, and I am proud to see you taking charge of your future in this way."

"Within reason," muttered Grandmama, which only caused Henrietta to giggle a second time.

"Nonsense. Now I know that you've insisted to me that wearing white and pretending to be bored are both hallmarks of town bronze, Henrietta, but neither of them suits you and never have. You're an engaging little minx whenever we're at home or with family, but out in society you're as forgettable as every other young miss that gets paraded out for Ton approval."

"Grandpapa!" she exclaimed, but he turned his hard gaze to hers.

"Don't you 'Grandpapa!' me, my girl. I've seen you bite your tongue from making a witty observation, or from engaging in a political argument, or correcting some buck whose understanding of scientific advancements is inferior to your own. Why you choose to hide your light is beyond me."

"But-" began Henrietta, but Grandmama cut her off before she could so much as utter a word in her own defence.

"And your Grandfather is quite correct about your wearing white, darling. It's not that it's an unbecoming colour on you as such, but it does nothing to enhance your complexion. It would be perfectly acceptable for us to inject some dark pinks or blues into your wardrobe, and perhaps to do something a bit more flattering with your hair."

"There's nothing wrong with my hair!" she exclaimed, starting to wish that she'd never started this conversation.

"Not if you were a governess," said Grandpapa, patting her on the shoulder. "But you're a beautiful young heiress who has been hiding her glory from the Ton for too long."

She glanced from one of them to the other, her gaze narrowing. "Why do I get the feeling that you're both enjoying this?"

Her grandparents stood, sharing another of those speaking looks as they did so.

"Why wouldn't we enjoy seeing our granddaughter finally want to shine?" said Grandmama. "Now let's call your maid in to see if we can't work some magic on your tresses before the ball this evening, and if we can use some of the acres of material in this house to liven up your gown."

As Grandmama crossed the room and pulled the rope to summon her maid, Grandpapa captured her hand and kissed her fingers in the way that was fashionable in his own youth.

"The boy is a fool," he said quietly, "and I will not allow you to bury yourself on his behalf for any longer."

Henrietta choked, and it was a good thing that he chose to leave at that moment, for she doubted that she could have said a single word to him without succumbing to more tears.

"Ellie, there you are," said Grandmama as Henrietta's maid entered the room. "I have simply wonderful news; Lady Henrietta has agreed to let us do something more fashionable with her hair. Do you have any suggestions?"

The look of happy anticipation on Ellie's face was so pronounced that Henrietta almost burst into laughter.

"Oh, yes, my Lady! I can think of several things we can do that'll really make the most of Lady Henrietta's strong cheekbones."

"And is it possible to give this evening's gown a dashing twist, do you think?"

Ellie's grin grew so wide it was as though an extra sun had appeared in the room. "It would be a pleasure to do so!"

The Marchioness smiled. "Excellent girl, I knew I could count on you. Now darling, you just need to sit there and rest your eyes while Ellie works her magic. We can't have you seen at the Loughcroft's ball with puffy eyes and tear-stained cheeks, now, can we?"

Good Lord, no, thought Henrietta as she did as she was bid. James will never know that I shed so much as a single tear over him.

*

Despite the Loughcroft's ball being early in the Season, it seemed as though the entire Ton had turned out with not so much as a single declined invitation. The spacious ballroom felt as though it was packed to the rafters with members of the Beau Monde with not so much as a foot of floor space was going spare. It was inevitable that the event would be rated a sad crush and intolerably hot all evening, thus setting an impossibly high standard for every ball, dance and supper party that was to follow in the coming months.

The Shropshires had dined with the family before the ball began, meaning that they were able to claim the best seats at the dance before the other, less important guests began to arrive. Henrietta's dance card quickly filled as she deliberately chose the best dancers among her acquaintance to lead her down into each set.

The first stage of her transformation was to discard the fashionable air of ennui that she had struggled to maintain since her come out, and instead to throw herself into the available entertainments with enthusiasm. Her friends Lady Cordelia and Miss Manning were both naturally gregarious, so it was surprisingly easy to laugh and smile as much as she dared, and even found herself enjoying the evening immensely, despite her conversation with James not five hours before.

It was amazing how much good dancing did for

a broken heart, she mused. Not all of her partners were the most entertaining of companions, but they had good legs, showed to advantage in their evening clothes, and were all quite happy to encourage her laughter and smiles.

Perhaps Grandpapa was right, she thought to herself as the music ended and her partner led her back the chairs beside her Grandmama. The evening is so much more enjoyable when you are willing to smile and laugh.

She did not have much time to mull over this revelation, however. Lord Loughcroft approached their group, bowing over her Grandmama's hand and paying the older woman such outlandish compliments that the Marchioness was compelled to rap his fingers with her fan.

"And what do you think of my Granddaughter's new style?" asked the Marchioness, only a slight tremor in her voice as Loughcroft turned his attention to Henrietta, quizzing glass already placed to his eye.

"Looking deuced pretty tonight, Henrietta," he said with a small nod of approval. "Far too much white as I keep on telling you, but the style of that gown combined with those ribbons give quite a romantic look to you, my dear."

Henrietta would have sworn that her Grandmama gave a sigh of relief. Loughcroft was a celebrated arbiter of fashion within the Ton, and he took his role seriously enough that her relationship with his wife would not save her from an honest and frank opinion. As such, a compliment from him was not something to be taken lightly.

"Thank you," she replied, secretly preening under his gaze. He took the empty chair beside her, stretching out his long legs as he looked her over once again.

"I particularly like what you've done with your hair, and I expect you'll have set a trend before the night is done."

"Do you really think so?" she asked, clutching the stem of her champagne glass so tightly she was afraid it would break.

Loughcroft grinned and lounged back a little further in his chair.

"Undoubtedly. The curls are much more in keeping with your real personality rather than the utterly bland style they try to encourage unmarried ladies to take. The dress is a bit simple for my tastes but - and forgive me for speaking bluntly here – it's a damn sight better than the debutante frills and furbelows you usually wear."

Henrietta chewed her lip, reminding herself that she would do well to listen to his advice, but unable to keep from defending herself.

"It's all the rage in the Lady's fashion magazines."

Loughcroft snorted. "Only if you want to sink into the ranks of all the other forgettable debutantes. That's not you and never has been. I'll be dashed if I understand why you'd want to appear so mild-mannered."

His words were uncomfortably close to those of her grandfather, and she took a sip of her champagne to stall for time before answering.

"I thought that was what a gentleman wanted in a wife?" she asked, her brows knitting together as Loughcroft gave a crack of laughter.

"Some gentlemen undoubtedly do, my dear, but tell me this: how many of them have you turned down now? Seven? Twelve?"

She felt her cheeks grow hot. "Only four," she muttered, and then took another, much longer mouthful of champagne as Loughcroft gave free rein to his mirth.

"Good grief, I had no idea it was that many! Wait until I tell Emma you've beaten her record – she'll be mortified."

"Well there's nothing to brag about in having multiple offers of marriage when you are disinclined to accept any of them," she replied.

"I wouldn't say that too loudly, my dear," said

Loughcroft, although his smile took any heat out of his words. "Not every woman is as fortunate as you in that regard."

Henrietta sighed. "I know I know; most ladies are not so fortunate as to have even one offer of marriage, and are doomed to be unpaid companions to their wealthier relatives. You are quite right, but the simple fact is I am an heiress, and I do not need to leg-shackle myself to the wrong man just because he asks me to marry him."

"Which of course begs the question: have you drawn the attention of the right man?"

Henrietta felt her blush deepen as Loughcroft laughed even louder, apparently uncaring about the attention he was drawing to them.

"I can't say I've met him yet," she lied, her eyes flicking over to the group of dancers beginning to gather before the band in preparation for the next dance. James was among their number, and on his arm was some pretty, demure little debutante who stared up into his eyes, entranced.

"And this change of style is to help you find the right gentleman for you, is it?"

"Is it so terribly obvious?" she asked, forcing herself to return her attention to her cousin's husband. Loughcroft simply smiled and took her hand in his, pulling her to her feet.

Henrietta looked quizzically at him as he led her away from the group of dancers. "Are we not partnered for the Cotillion?"

"We are, but your campaign is of greater importance, and besides, we need reinforcements," he said, before leading her through the crowds of guests and toward his wife.

Emma, looking glorious in a dark red dress that Henrietta immediately coveted, turned to her with a radiant smile.

"Henrietta, my darling girl, are you enjoying yourself? Frightful squeeze, isn't it? I'm desperately afraid that we'll run out of champagne," said Emma as she bussed her on the cheek. The Loughcrofts had only recently returned to town with their bouncing baby in tow, and Henrietta had to admit that motherhood seemed to agree with her cousin; Emma didn't glow so much as she radiated love and beauty. It was at once both wondrous and deeply depressing.

"Your faith in my ability to stock our cellars never fails to warm my heart," replied Loughcroft with a world-weary sigh. "I suppose nothing I say will reassure you until the morning when all the guests have left, and we still have enough wine in the house to flood the city."

Emma cast a glance at her husband that was half exasperation, half adoration, and Henrietta knew a pang of envy.

This is what I want for myself, she thought. This is what I need.

"I have to say you're looking monstrously pretty this evening, Coz," said Emma, looking over Henrietta with the same appreciative eye that her husband had used earlier. "You simply have to tell me how you did your hair like that; I'd swear those curls are about to tumble loose any moment, and yet you've danced the night away so far with nary a stray hair."

"I'm hoping to move from the ranks of demure miss into those of the ravishing heiresses," she confided in a rush, her voice sounding far weaker than she'd hoped for.

Emma and Alistair shared another glance before her cousin tucked Henrietta's arm into her own.

"I think I shall go and sit out on the balcony for the rest of this set, my dear," declared Emma. "I shall steal you away from my husband to keep me company before I faint dead away with the heat. Loughcroft, go do something about it."

The Viscount gave a long-suffering sigh. "Of course, my love, I shall go call upon the Greek god of the weather to set us up a light breeze." He executed a graceful bow and then disappeared back into the crowds.

"He does know that there were multiple Greek weather gods, doesn't he?" Henrietta asked as they made their way to the balcony.

"Highly doubtful; Alistair once told me that he thought the Ancient Gods were a 'dashed havey-cavey bunch of individuals, especially the one with the duck'."

There was a brief pause as Henrietta tried to think of an intelligent response, and failed.

"I'm not sure I know which god he is referring to," she said faintly, but Emma just shrugged.

"I think he meant when Zeus turned into a swan to seduce Leda, but when I asked him, he turned bright red and refused to discuss it any further."

"How... interesting," said Henrietta, trying very hard not to laugh.

"That's Alistair for you. Now, let's sit down on this bench to cool ourselves, and you can tell me precisely why you've decided to drop this Perfect Young Miss routine. Have you given up on Lord Cottingham completely?"

"Who said that I was holding out on Lord Cottingham's regard?" said Henrietta, her voice an entire pitch higher than normal.

"You told me when you were ten that you were

going to marry him, and have an annoying habit of adding the phrase 'but James says' in front of roughly half your arguments for everything up to and including wearing very proper but heart-wrenchingly boring dresses."

"Perhaps when I was ten, I said such things, but that is hardly reflective of my current beliefs."

"You used the phrase this Christmas, and he wasn't even there."

"No, he wasn't," said Henrietta, and she felt her shoulders droop even as her traitorous eyes filled with tears. "He was in Canada on a grand adventure, and – oh Emma, he didn't even miss me one bit."

"Darling don't cry," said Emma, sounding alarmed as she threw her arm about Henrietta and drew her closer. "I'm sure that he thought about you."

"Not once. Not even enough to send me a note, or bring me a gift, or even to read any of my letters. I only saw him this afternoon because he saw fit to call on Grandmama, and then decided to tell me that it was high time I should think about finding a husband – just not him, apparently."

"What a perfect nincompoop," pronounced Emma. "Evidently he's deaf, dumb and blind."

"Be that as it may, it dawned on me after his visit that I've wasted four years trying to be his version of the ideal bride: genteel, kind, demure, and all that boring rot until I've turned into a prosy old bore."

"The prosiest," agreed Emma, causing Henrietta to look up and glare at her older cousin.

"You're supposed to be helping."

"But it's only the truth, darling – you've squashed your character, vivacity and intellect into a perfect little package of white muslin, and in the process, you've lost all the most interesting things about you. Why, the only time I've seen you come alive of late was during the snowball fight at Shropshire Hall, where you ambushed George and dumped him in a snowbank."

Henrietta couldn't help but smile at that memory. "I'd waited years to do that, you know."

"Precisely. That's the real Henrietta that we all know and love, not the cow-eyed ninny who sits in the corner and utters inane small talk."

"You really aren't pulling your punches, are you?"

Emma gave an exasperated sigh. "I'm sorry, but it's about time you heard it. Tell me truthfully; has Lord Cottingham ever complimented you on your demure demeanour?"

She considered the question, sure that there was at least one point where he had done so, but came up blank. "No, I suppose not."

"And has he ever berated you for any of your harebrained escapades, or called you out on that shocking temper of yours?"

"He did once call me a hoyden when I was twelve, but then I'd stolen his clothes while he was swimming and dumped them into the lake," said Henrietta, but even then she knew it didn't count.

"You see? Even Lord Cottingham doesn't truly believe you have to be some colourless milksop."

"Well I don't care about what James thinks any longer," said Henrietta, but after meeting Emma's piercing gaze, she added: "at least, I don't want to care. Dearest, I'm so tired of being a milksop, as you so kindly put it. I want to be dashing like you are. I don't want to be courted by these properly dull gentlemen who make me want to run from the room screaming just to escape them. I can't go all the way to Canada like James did, but that doesn't mean that I don't want a bit of adventure of my own."

"That's the spirit!"

"Which is why I want you to help me."

"I thought you'd never ask. I'll take you shopping tomorrow, and we'll have you tricked out in the brightest of colours in no time."

"You are an absolute diamond."

"I know, and it's about time this family started to appreciate me more."

Henrietta gave her a squeeze. "Best of cousins! I shall endeavour to take your side in all future family arguments, and will dump your brother in a snowbank next winter just to prove my devotion to you."

"You might have to come up with an alternative plan; it's rare you can catch out George with the same trick twice. I-" she paused suddenly as something on the far side of the room caught her attention. "Good Lord, he actually came!"

Henrietta turned to look in the same direction, but could not see who had drawn her cousin's attention.

"Who, your brother?"

"No, George and Abby won't be returning to town for another few weeks yet. My dear, I'm going to escort you back to your Grandmama, then there is someone I simply must go talk to."

"Oh, well, of course you must not neglect your guests," said Henrietta, feeling slightly put out.

Emma only laughed. "Hush you silly goose, I have a very good idea on how to help you, but I need to speak with an old friend first."

Henrietta frowned. "Emma, are you scheming?

Remember how at Christmas you swore most faithfully that you were going to stop playing matchmaker at every opportunity?"

"I remember nothing of the sort," lied Emma. "Besides, my scheming always comes together in the end – look at how happy my brother is!"

"They ran off and got married in secret," Henrietta felt compelled to point out. "And so did Captain Rowlands and Charlotte Harden."

Emma nodded. "Yes, and look how spectacularly well that all worked out. Trust me, Coz. Have a little faith."

The only problem with that, thought Henrietta, was that putting your faith in Emma was rather like trusting in the sun to shine at a picnic.

CHAPTER THREE

James kept an inane smile plastered to his face as he counted down the minutes for the dance to end. Miss Juneberry, while very pretty and a tolerable dancer, apparently lacked even one ounce of personality. She answered every question with meaningless pleasantries, suffered from the requisite amount of ennui to be fashionable, and yet retained a mild enthusiasm befitting for her station in life.

In short, she was identical to every other young woman he had danced with this evening. The moment the band finished he walked her back to her family as quickly as possible, made some inane pleasantries of his own and then escaped to the sanctuary of his mother, the dowager Lady Cottingham, and the Marchioness.

"What a lovely set of young ladies this year's

debutantes are showing themselves to be," said his mother as he collapsed into the chair beside her. "Such perfect manners, and so very pretty."

"Yes, I suppose so," said James, struggling to conjure up even a jot of enthusiasm.

"And such very good dancers," added Lady Shropshire as she fanned herself. "The current fashions certainly make it easier for them to look elegant during a country dance than it did during my own youth. It must be a real pleasure for you, James."

"Yes," he replied, but his lack of enthusiasm was not lost on the older ladies.

"Is something wrong, my dear?" asked his mother, her thin face creased up in concern. "Were you not looking forward to meeting so many eligible young women at one place?"

"I'm sure they're all very nice young ladies," said James, glad that there were no gossipy matchmakers nearby to overhear his mother's turn of phrase.

"Are you finally hunting for a wife, my dear boy?" asked Lady Shropshire, snapping her fan shut and placing it into her lap. She was regarding him with an intensity that he wasn't sure he liked, and it was with great effort that he resisted tugging at his cravat.

"No no, well at least, I'm not actively hunting, but Mother pointed out to me on my return from

Canada that I'm about to turn twenty-five, and it is time I at least started considering the future of the estate. Still, it's not like I'm in my dotage, so there's plenty of time yet."

"I disagree," said the Marchioness, slapping his knuckles with her fan. "As I was just telling your mother, this romantic nonsense about marrying for love is far too prevalent these days. Why I barely knew the Marquis when I married him, but our affection grew and matured with time. You would do well to follow suit, and marry a girl that you held in esteem and affection."

"I said something similar to Henry," replied James, wondering why it didn't feel quite so edifying to be on the receiving end of such practical advice.

"Did you?" said Lady Shropshire in an odd tone that made him look up at her quizzically.

"Yes, when we were chatting this afternoon. She told me about her four offers, and I suggested that she'd be better off choosing someone with whom she shared mutual respect rather than thinking some reformed rake would sweep her off her feet and fall madly in love with her."

The Marchioness looked shocked, and he wondered if perhaps he'd overstepped the mark. "That explains so much," she murmured.

Before he could inquire as to her precise meaning, his mother gave a dramatic sigh. "James, that was very poorly done of you."

He frowned, not entirely sure what either of the ladies were talking about.

"It was just some friendly advice, well-intentioned," he said in his own defence, but his mother glanced at the Marchioness – a woman old enough to be her mother, and shook her head as if to say, "children."

There was no opportunity to pursue the conversation, however, as Henry chose that moment to return to her Grandmama's side. She was arm-in-arm with the dapper Lord Loughcroft, and even James wasn't so dense as to be unaware of the fact she was looking positively radiant.

"Fabulous party, isn't it?" announced Henry in a loud voice. "I've been telling Loughcroft that he and Emma have done us all a monstrous disservice in hosting this squeeze, for how can we possibly compete?"

"I suggested that someone should turn their ballroom into Astley's Amphitheatre," said Loughcroft with his signature smile. "I thought it would be a capital theme for this little gathering, but Emma vetoed the suggestion. I still think it would make a simply cracking party, don't you Cottingham?"

"It would certainly be memorable," laughed James,

partly at the look of horror on his mother's face. "I'm willing to consider it for our own ball."

"That's splendid!" laughed Henry, and James found himself wondering when he'd last seen her looking so happy. "Instead of dancing, the young debutantes shall have to perform riding tricks like the Equestriennes. May I volunteer myself for the first set?"

James smiled at her, reminded forcefully of the girl who used to romp through wet fields with him just because she wanted to feed his horses a treat.

"You'd have to convince me that you can control a horse well enough to allow it in my ballroom," he said, and grinned at the look of shocked disgust on her face.

"Of all the shabby things to say when you know I'm an excellent rider!"

"Riding sedately alongside your Grandmama in her landaulet doesn't count," he replied, intending it to be a light-hearted piece of banter, but his laugh died as he caught the moment of sheer fury in her eyes before she quickly hid it behind a wall of false cheerfulness.

"Then perhaps you should pay more attention, Lord Cottingham," Henry replied with a smile that on anyone else he would have believed to be genuine. "Riding is still a favoured pastime of mine."

"Indeed, her grandfather is always happy to brag that our darling girl has a good seat," said Lady Shropshire as she began to fan herself once again. "Henry is accomplished in many things, but she shows to perfection when galloping through the countryside, or tooling about in her gig."

The compliment, although casual, had an interesting impact on Henry. She visibly softened as she turned a warm gaze onto her grandmother. "That means the world, coming from such an accomplished horsewoman like yourself."

"I may not be able to ride much anymore," said the Marchioness, "but I trust that my skill with a carriage is beyond reproach and that I have taught Henry to drive with precision and grace."

"It's certainly a family accomplishment," said James' mother, holding a hand out to Henry. "It has always been a pleasure to have you tool me about in your gig when we are in the country. You simply must treat me to a drive here in London; I can't think as to why I haven't requested it before."

"Alas I do not have a suitable carriage in town, but I promise most faithfully to take you out when we are all back home," smiled Henry, a look of genuine pleasure on her face.

James glanced at each of the three women in turn, trying to decipher whatever deeper communication was going on about him. In desperation, he looked up at Lord Loughcroft for guidance, but that gentleman seemed to be intently examining his cuff with what looked suspiciously like a smirk.

Thankfully the band signalled the formation of the supper dance, a waltz that he had promised to Henry only that afternoon. He got to his feet and held out his arm to her, glad that the dance would allow them to converse, and give him the opportunity to make up for the hurt he had caused over her letters.

"Shall we?" he asked with good cheer that was only slightly tempered by the hesitation in his oldest friend. No doubt he'd bruised her feelings with the comment about her ability as a horsewoman, but surely a dance and some supper would repair their relationship.

"Henrietta, may I introduce you to one of my oldest friends?" came a commanding female voice. Lady Loughcroft approached on the arm of a man he did not recognise. The swarthy gentleman was undoubtedly a wealthy aristocrat based on his clothes and demeanour, and in his early thirties at least. James had not seen him on the town in the five years he had been attending London for the Season, nor at any of the house parties organised by his acquaintances over the summer and autumn months.

"Your Grace, this is my cousin, Lady Henrietta Cartwright. She wasn't out last time you were down for the Season, which is why I haven't had the honour of introducing you before. Henry, this is the Duke of Devenish, an old friend of mine and Gloucester, and he is keen to make your acquaintance."

"A pleasure," said the Duke, bowing deeply.

It was all James could do to stop his mouth from falling open. This was the Devilish Duke, as the papers had christened him? The man had had his name linked with many a flighty widow over the years, and not a few married women as well. He had fought several duels over his inamoratas, and had left so many broken hearts among the unmarried misses of the Ton that he was widely considered to be dangerous.

So why in the name of all that was holy was Lady Loughcroft introducing an unapologetic rake to Henry?

"Good Lord, is that really you, Devenish?" exclaimed the Marchioness, sitting up straighter. "I thought you'd sworn off London forever after your last misadventure."

The Duke inclined his head toward the older Lady. "Indeed I did, my Lady, but in order to convince my mother to visit with Dr Knight, she demanded my return to society as payment."

"The Duchess is in London? How wonderful! I would love to call on her if she is receiving?"

"How could we refuse a visit from such a dear friend as the Marchioness of Shropshire?" said Devenish, capturing her hand and kissing the air an inch above her fingers. "Of course, I demand a price for letting my mother know that you are desirous of a social call."

Much to James' astonishment, Lady Shropshire chuckled. "You always were an insolent wretch. Tell me then, what are your demands?"

The Duke pretended to consider. "Is a waltz with you too much to request?"

"You know it is, puppy! Besides, with your reputation, the Marquis would likely call you out, and it would be the Rothman incident all over again."

The Duke held his hand across his heart. "You wound me, my dear Lady."

"You'll recover I'm sure," said Lady Shropshire tartly, although the effect was ruined by her obvious enjoyment of the exchange.

The Duke turned his eyes toward Henry and reached a hand toward her. "What do you say, Lady Henrietta? Will you help heal my wounded heart by dancing this waltz with me?"

James smirked, expecting Henry to politely rebuff the Duke and to take her place in the waltz with him, or for the Marchioness to decline on her behalf.

Instead, Henry took the Duke's hand into hers, a becoming blush in her cheeks as she accepted his offer. "I can hardly leave you nursing such terrible heartache only moments after returning to the Ton, Your Grace."

"Henry!" was all James could think of to splutter as the Duke began to lead her away to the dance floor. His friend glanced at him over her shoulder.

"You don't mind, do you, James? After all, it's not like we haven't danced together a thousand times before."

He stared at her, his mouth opening and closing as he failed to find the right words to express his thoughts on the matter.

Another arm linked with his, and he found himself looking into the smiling eyes of Lady Loughcroft. "I am so sorry, I had no notion that you were to dance this set with my cousin. Come, let me make amends; ah Miss Hemsworth, would you please help me out of a pickle and partner my dear friend Lord Cottingham for the Waltz?"

James found himself bowing to a pale-skinned girl in a lace dress, who looked frighteningly like every other single young lady he had found himself dancing with that evening.

"Your servant, Miss Hemsworth," he said, and the girl responded with some simpering comment as he led her out to join the set.

He plastered a smile on his face, wondering how he was going to get through the rest of the evening.

*

"I'm so very pleased to make your acquaintance, Your Grace," said Henrietta as the Duke swept her around the room to a beautiful waltz.

"The pleasure is all mine," he smiled back at her, his grin decidedly wolfish. She'd heard all about him, of course; who hadn't been told the stories of the Devilish Duke? A man who was regarded as a Corinthian by half of London's male population, and as a veritable god by the rest. His wealth made her own sizeable fortune look paltry, and he was not afraid to spend his money on anything from a bang-up bit of blood to an enamelled snuffbox.

The epithet Devilish, however, came more from his wicked sense of humour than anything else – or at least that was what Grandpapa had told her years ago when he first left London, and Grandpapa had known the Duke since he was born.

Of course, he wasn't precisely an angel, either. His enemies had a habit of becoming the victim of outrageous pranks or losing their fortune. His biggest danger, however, was to bold young debutantes with their hearts set on becoming the next Duchess of Devenish. He'd been known to court ambitious young maidens with flair and panache, publicly setting up expectations of a marriage proposal – only to forget the girl's name the following day, and to act as though they had never been introduced.

Many condemned him for this behaviour, but Henrietta had considerable sympathy for the man.

"I suppose Emma forced you to dance with me," she said and was rewarded by an amused smile.

"You don't believe in beating around the bush, do you?"

"I don't want you to think that you're being coerced into courting me," she explained. "I love my cousin to pieces, but she can be a trifle meddling when it comes to affairs of the heart."

"She is indeed meddling on your behalf, but I was perfectly willing to accept my role in this drama. By the by, do you have any idea how adorable you look when you blush?"

She giggled. "Now I know you are bamming me! I've been reliably informed that I turn the colour of an overripe tomato."

"But tomatoes are both enticing and delectable," he replied with a grin she suspected had set hearts fluttering the length and breadth of England.

She couldn't help but giggle again. "You are a complete hand, Your Grace!"

He gave a chest-deep sigh, his face the picture of a wounded swain. "Do you doubt my sincerity, Lady Henrietta? Would you believe me if I told you that I fell head over heels in love with you the moment I set eyes upon you this evening and demanded Emma introduce me to the mate of my very soul?"

"Codswallop," she said. His eyes widened for just a moment, and then the Duke through his head back in a loud roar of manly laughter.

He was also an excellent dancer, for he did not miss so much as a single step in their waltz.

"You, my dear Lady Henrietta, are a delight."

She smiled. "Are you going to tell me the truth, now? How did Emma coerce you into dancing with me?"

"Your cousin once came to my rescue in an incident I really have no wish to recollect, but needless to say she was a perfect heroine, and we have been friends ever since."

"Was she meddling?"

"Absolutely. However, it was to my benefit, and her meddling has a very annoying habit of paying off."

Henrietta couldn't stop her rueful grin. "It does, doesn't it? And she's always so insufferable about it afterwards. But why, precisely, has her meddling brought us together for this waltz?"

"Ah, it will be for far more than this one waltz, Lady Henrietta. I believe I am to make you all the crack and help you to bring the menfolk of London to their knees in worship."

Henrietta laughed. "Are you even capable of being serious? I would be perfectly content with meeting some interesting gentlemen who are intelligent, witty and kind. Even one would be enough."

"Just one gentleman at your feet? Was there someone, in particular, you had in mind?"

She didn't trust herself to answer, so tried to look arch and aloof, even though she knew she failed miserably on both counts. The Duke cocked his head to one side, studying her with an intensity that made her feel as though he had ripped open her heart and understood all her darkest secrets.

"Definitely just one gentleman, then. Ah, don't look so unhappy; the first rule of being dashing, my dear, is never to look sad when doing something scandalous."

"But we aren't doing anything scandalous."

"You're waltzing with the Devilish Duke, who intends to remain glued to your side throughout supper and to lead you out into the following set. I shall refuse to dance with any other woman, and will stare at you for the rest of the evening in a brooding-yet-handsome manner. I've been told that I'm awfully good at that. Believe me, Lady Henrietta, you will be the talk of the town by morning as a result."

"You're very sure of yourself," she replied, struggling to keep a smile from her lips.

"The Ton is a game, and I am a master player, my dear. Am I to know the young gentleman who you wish to have fallen at your feet? Before you answer, throw your head back and laugh as though I have told you the most delicious joke; we are about to pass by Lady Harden, and the Old Bat is the biggest gossip in London."

Henrietta did as she was bid, and was rewarded by a smile that would be devastating if it wasn't so obviously calculated.

"I made the mistake of trying to be the perfect, demure young lady," she replied, deciding that honesty would be the best course with this man. "All that happened is I've attracted the attention of some perfectly dull gentlemen, or men who think that they will be able to control my fortune after marriage. As for the man I thought I wanted... well, he does not love me, so I think it is best for me to cast a net into more interesting waters."

"And you think being dashing will help that? I can assure you from personal experience that it does not."

"But at least you have fun," she pointed out. "If I'm going to be saddled with offers from gentlemen only interested in my fortune and good birth, I might as well enjoy myself."

The music came to an end, leaving Henrietta surprised at how fast the time had passed. She took the Duke's proffered arm, and they made their way through to the supper room. Naturally, he secured the best table, and once she was seated, he made sure to stare into her eyes as though he was truly besotted with her.

"I wholeheartedly agree with you, Lady Henrietta, as does your cousin. It seems to me that whoever you were trying to impress with this Perfect Miss act of yours wasn't worth the trouble."

Henrietta couldn't help but glance across at a nearby table, where James was sitting with a demure young lady with perfect brown curls and large, adoring eyes.

"No he wasn't," she lied, then turned her attention back to the Duke, who was looking at her with that same intensity again that she found so uncomfortable.

"I am happy to help you have a little more fun

during this Season, Lady Henrietta, and your family connections combined with your fortune, will protect you from the worst of the gossipmongers. I will even make sure that you are introduced to gentlemen whose interests are more in line with your own than your previous suitors. But in return, you must agree that you will be guided by me as to what is too close to the line and what is bad Ton, for Emma will never forgive me if I allow you to stray into the realms of the vulgar."

Henrietta shuddered at the thought. "Nothing is further than my intentions than that! Very well, Your Grace; when can we get started?"

He captured her hand and placed a firm kiss on her fingers, making her gasp in surprise. "My dear, the games have already begun."

CHAPTER FOUR

"How are you enjoying being back in England, James?" asked Henrietta as her old friend drove her around Hyde Park at an hour deemed ungodly by most of the Ton. It was a revival of an old tradition of theirs, where they had taken a drive through the park before much of the Beau Monde was awake and their days began in earnest.

"Very much; I was surprised at how much I missed the hubbub of London and being close to my family. I even missed some of my friends – not that I'd admit it to them! William and Herbert would never let me live it down if they thought I'd felt deprived of their company."

She winced a touch at his words, but as he was focussed so much on his horses, he didn't seem to notice. They were from his own stable rather than hired hacks; a beautiful match pair of bays that would no doubt draw many envious looks through-out the season.

Although he was only driving a gig rather than a more fashionable Phaeton, it was a well-hung vehicle with a smart blue body that was more than pleasant to ride in for an afternoon jaunt. He drove the horses tandem which led a slightly rakish air to the setup, and had she not known that his bays were as docile as a pair of sleepy cows she would have been quite impressed with his driving.

Henrietta's hands were itching to take hold of the reins and to drive for herself. She missed her own little gig and the sense of freedom it afforded her.

Finally, she could stand it no more.

"I wish you would let me take the reins, James. There's barely another person in sight, so I'm not going to cause an accident even if I did manage to forget everything Grandpapa taught me."

"Sorry, Henry, not going to happen no matter how much you wheedle. These bays are my pride and joy, not to mention that driving in London is a little different to tooling about in the country."

"We're in Hyde Park," she said, irritated and exasperated all at once, "and besides, I've driven Grandpapa's barouche through Mayfair before now, so I'm hardly incompetent."

"Be that as it may, it's not like you drive as much as you used to, and I'm not trusting them to a less-than-experienced pair of hands. You can take Lord Shropshire's horses out whenever the fancy takes you - I'm still not trusting you with mine!"

Henrietta quietly but firmly folded her hands in her lap so she could resist the urge to punch him. Good grief, had he always been this condescending?

No, she answered herself immediately. No, he hadn't.

Before her come out, he'd thought her a capital rider and complimented her driving regularly - even going so far as to say it was a pity the Four in Hand club wouldn't allow females into their ranks. Since then he'd seen her riding sedately around the park with her various suitors or with her grandparents, or on a rare occasion, driving her own gig over to visit his mother, who she took out with her at a considerably gentler pace than she took when she was alone. It was not surprising that he had lost his faith in her ability to drive. Presented with the same evidence in the other direction, she would undoubtedly have lost her faith in him.

And yet it rankled. It hurt that he believed she would just somehow forget all the lessons her Grandpapa had given her, or that she would suddenly cease to love the freedom of a drive the way she had at sixteen. He should have known.

Just a year ago she'd been pining for the opportunity to ride out with him just like this, but imagining all sorts of wonderful reunions where they would laugh out loud and he would compliment her light hand on the reins, before taking the opportunity to confess his undying love for her.

How much has changed in a twelvemonth, she thought, and sighed for the pity of it.

"Tuckered out, are you?" said James, seemingly mistaking her sigh for a yawn. "I'm not surprised with the way you've been gadding about for the last week. I never knew you had so much energy, dancing every set at every ball!"

"What better way to get to know eligible gentlemen?" she asked, keeping her tone light. "I'm hardly going to meet my future husband by deliberately playing the wallflower, now am I?"

"Well yes I suppose that's a fair enough point, but I feel like I've barely had a chance to catch up with you since my return," he said.

Henrietta stared at him for a long moment. "Are you reprimanding me for not making time for you?"

"Well, I have been out of the country for a year, Henry," he replied. "I don't think it's too much to ask that you make a little bit of time to fill me in on everything I've missed."

"I have made time for you," she snapped. "I'm

here right now, am I not? Considering you did not do me the courtesy of informing me of your return to England, I had made other arrangements with my friends for entertainment. This might surprise you, James, but I don't spend my time sitting around pining for you when you aren't here."

"Don't cut up rough at me," he laughed, which only served to fuel the cold anger building in her stomach. "You're right, I'm sure your time is very much in demand by the Ton, and I'm sorry for suggesting otherwise."

Henrietta closed her eyes and took a series of deep, steadying breaths. Of all the infuriating, condescending, irritating men she'd ever known! Was this the effect of travelling abroad, or inheriting the title, or had he always been like this?

She opened her eyes and plastered a smile onto her face. "Well as you said, you have been out of the country for a year, so I cannot blame you for being unaware of my status within the Beau Monde. Now that I'm taking this husband-hunting seriously, it means I have even less time available for trivial things like a morning drive."

James finally looked over at her. "Steady on, Henry, there's no need to get up in your high ropes."

Henrietta laughed and patted his hand. "Don't worry, you're still my childhood friend, and always will be. Now, is it true that Lord Standish is considering matrimony? I know Herbert Filey is, but as sweet as he can be, I'm afraid we wouldn't suit in the long run."

"You and Herbert? Good God, no!"

"Yes, that was my thought – and it is his fault that I'm subjected to awful poetry. Lord Standish, on the other hand, is a great gun, and I imagine that marriage to him would be something of an adventure."

James looked slightly sick. "Henry, stop it. You know very well that you and William wouldn't suit."

"I disagree," she said lightly, "but I promised to take your opinion into consideration and so I will. Besides, he doesn't hold a candle to Devenish."

"Don't tell me that you're allowing that rogue to court you?"

Henrietta managed to keep her smile serene, although she enjoyed seeing him so put out of joint. "The Duke has shown every consideration and has singled me out for his attention over the past week. In fact, we are to go riding together tomorrow, and then we will both be attending a rather select card party with the Jerseys that evening."

Her friend looked troubled. "Henry, you do know that his nickname is Devilish, don't you?"

She laughed, although it sounded alarmingly

like a titter even to her own ears. "I know, such a droll play on his title! His father and mine were friends, you know, and Grandpapa is very pleased to see our families renew their ties."

Her words had the desired effect as she watched his knuckles turn white, the reins tight in his fists.

"I suppose there is no point in warning you away from the Duke if Lord and Lady Shropshire are encouraging your new... friendship."

"No, I don't suppose there is," she agreed. "You need to loosen your grip, James. You don't want to ruin their mouths by being too rough with them. After all, they are your pride and joy."

"I don't need advice on driving, thank you," he said, but she glanced pointedly at his hands.

James turned the gig and headed out of Hyde Park at the earliest opportunity, cutting their time together short by a good ten minutes. Henrietta didn't comment and instead prattled on about her plans to go shopping with her cousin Emma to smarten up her wardrobe, as well as to spend more time with the fashionable Lady Cordelia and her cousin, Miss Manning.

"How interesting," James said politely from time to time, or sometimes "Indeed!"

She knew he was barely listening and wasn't sure if she was angry or amused at his reaction.

They turned onto Hanover Square, leaving little time to needle him before he pulled up before the Shropshire mansion.

"Of course, Devenish is taking me out driving next week," she lied, "and I am quite looking forward to his teaching me to drive four-in-hand."

"Then he's more of a fool than I thought," snapped James as he brought his horses to a standstill, "for I wouldn't trust you with a curricle and pair."

The callousness served to both hurt and anger her. She looked him up and down before casually raising a single brow. "Is that so? Then perhaps it is for the best that I will be in the care of a noted nonpareil than a mere country whipster. Good day to you, Lord Cottingham."

She stepped down from the carriage, a waiting footman already there to help her descend.

"Henry!"

She had not intended to stop before she was safely inside her home, but she could not ignore the entreaty. She turned and looked up at James as he ran a hand through his dark brown locks.

"Yes?" she said.

James shook his head, something like confusion on his face as he glanced toward the footman first, and then back to her.

"Is everything all right between us?" he eventually asked.

She held his gaze for a long while, commanding herself that neither a smile nor tears would show.

"Everything is the same as it ever was," she replied.

And was somewhat disgusted to see that he was relieved by her answer.

He relaxed his shoulders and then smiled at her. "We always did bicker, didn't we? Shall I see you at Lady Putney's ball? Save me a dance of some kind."

He threw a careless wave in her direction before setting his horses to and driving away out of Hanover Square.

Henrietta realised that she was shaking, and stuffed both hands firmly into her muff so that the footman would not see. She entered her home and had just passed her hat and pelisse to the butler when Grandpapa appeared in the hallway.

"Hello my dear, did you enjoy your drive out with Cottingham?" he asked.

"Yes, it was pleasant," she replied with as wide a smile as she could conjure.

Grandpapa was not fooled. He looked her up and down quickly and then held out a hand to his side.

"Come into the library and tell me everything."

Within moments, Henrietta found herself curled up in her favourite leather chair with a glass of ratafia gripped firmly between her fingers, her muff discarded at her feet. Grandpapa took his customary seat on the opposite side of the fire, his clear eyes looking her over as he waited for her to confide in him.

"James doesn't think I can handle his horses," she blurted out when she could no longer stand it.

Grandpapa gazed at her, one eyebrow raised in a way she hoped that she could imitate.

"His bays?"

She nodded.

"High Steppers, very showy and well matched," said Grandpapa, his head cocked to one side as he considered them. "However there's not an ounce of spirit in either of them. Perfect if you want a sedate ride around the city, but not at all suitable for a lively young woman like yourself."

Henrietta smiled. "Does that mean I'm allowed to ride Cassidus?"

"Not if you want to live," replied Grandpapa without so much as a blink. "Even in my prime, I would have struggled to manage that brute. No, my dear girl, I mean that it's high time you had some horseflesh of your own."

"I have Iris," she replied, feeling compelled to come to the defence of her striking black filly. "She's more heart than half the horses in London."

Grandpapa chuckled. "I know, my dear – I helped to birth her!"

"And we've never had better from your stables," said Henrietta, meaning every word. Her smile faded, and she frowned. "But sometimes, I want to drive."

Grandpapa flicked open his snuff-box and helped himself to a pinch. He sneezed, and then dabbed at his nose with his handkerchief.

"You can take out the barouche so long as you let me know in advance, my dear," he said.

"Yes, I know, and I appreciate it," she said. "I may even have to offer my services as coachman to Grandmama just to prove that I'm quite adept at driving many different carriages."

Grandpapa smiled but didn't comment.

The clock on the mantelpiece began to chime, making Henrietta jump.

"Good grief, is that the time? Emma will be here at any moment to take me shopping – I must go and ready myself.

"One must never waste time in matters of fashion," said Grandpapa. "Be off with you, dear heart – but give me a kiss first."

Henrietta laughed and planted a kiss on her grandfather's cheek. It wasn't until much later that she considered how thoughtful he had seemed, but dismissed it. Horses were always a serious business where Lord Shropshire was concerned.

*

Henry had changed, and for the life of him, James could not figure out how or why.

He considered the matter as he drove home. Ever since his return from Canada, she had been up in her high ropes as if constantly looking for a reason to be offended. Trying to tease her into a good mood the way he had when they were children only served to set her back up, and God forbid he actually try to gently correct her on something!

Women, he thought with an exasperated sigh, because as hard as it was to accept, Henry was a woman now and no longer the hoyden he'd grown up with.

The thought caught him off guard, and he frowned at it. Henry was certainly a woman in her twenties now – practically on the shelf – but her behaviour over the last week had been more reminiscent of his childhood friend that the demure young miss of the past three years. Not once had she asked him for the chance to drive his horses since she was sixteen, but the Henry of old had begged him at every opportunity – and even had the audacity to steal his gig one memorable summer.

"I'd forgotten about that," he murmured to himself, and was still chuckling at the memory of the anarchy she'd caused in the local village as he pulled up at the mews behind his home. He handed his horses and gig to the care of his stable hand before wandering through the gardens and up to the servant entrance to his townhome. Cook and the maids curtseyed briefly but otherwise paid him no heed at all as he made his way through the kitchens and out to the main hallway.

Although a considerably smaller property that the Shropshire's mansion on Hanover Square, he was proud of his smart Mayfair address and well-appointed home. He nodded a greeting to the butler and footmen before striding up the stairs, intending to clean himself up and prepare for a leisurely stroll down to his club.

"James, you are home!" cried his mother as he stepped onto the first-floor landing. He winced but was too well mannered to pretend that he had not heard her. He backtracked and entered the room, bowing deeply to his mother and her guests.

"Good morning, ladies," he said to the room as

a whole, and was surprised that it invoked laughter from at least one of the occupants.

"La, to fancy a baron mistaking me for a Lady! I'm just plain Mrs Juneberry – although my husband is descended from an Earl on his mother's side, of course," laughed an older woman as she came up from a deep curtsey. "You remember my daughter Amelia no doubt, from the Loughcroft's ball."

"Assuredly," he lied, smiling at a plump, pretty girl who he had nothing more than a vague recollection of dancing with. "How do you do, Miss Juneberry?"

"Very well, my Lord," she replied quietly, her eyes not quite meeting his.

"The Juneberrys were so good as to call on me this morning, and we've been enjoying a comfortable coze," said his mother with an encouraging smile at her guests. James cocked one eyebrow in her direction, knowing full well that Lady Cottingham, for all her many positive attributes, was an inveterate snob who considered women like Mrs Juneberry to be encroaching mushrooms.

"My Lady is too kind," simpered Mrs Juneberry, "and has made so many lovely compliments about my Amelia that I'm sure her head will be turned! Not that she isn't deserving of them, of course, but then you must forgive a mother's indulgence when it comes to believing that her daughter is a diamond of the first water!"

James smiled, and felt a flash of pity for Miss Juneberry as her mother's words caused her to blush.

"Your daughter is certainly on par with the other debutantes that I have had the pleasure of meeting with," he said with perfect truth.

"You see, Amelia?" crowed Mrs Juneberry. "What a pretty compliment to be paid to you, and from such a handsome peer, nonetheless!"

"You are too kind, my Lord," said Miss Juneberry, but from her expression, James guessed she was intelligent enough to realise that he had not really paid her a compliment at all.

"James dearest, Miss Juneberry was just telling me about how much she likes the theatre, so I have invited them to attend with us next week. Won't that be wonderful?" said his mother, leaving him no polite way to decline her suggestion. He threw her a speaking look, but her attention had been commanded by her teacup.

"What a nice idea," he said without much enthusiasm, "I'm sure it will be a pleasant enough evening."

"I'm sure it will be quite marvellous," declared Mrs Juneberry, "and will allow you to get to know my darling Amelia all the better until perhaps you find her as darling as I do."

Her darling Amelia closed her eyes in what James suspected was a silent prayer for deliverance. He found himself in sympathy, for since glaring at his mother wasn't working, he was making a silent pray of his own.

CHAPTER FIVE

"I am most perfectly convinced that you are a nonpareil when it comes to driving, my dear Lady Henrietta, but on no account will I be teaching you to drive four in hand!" said Devenish, his tone laced with bemusement as they strolled through the high stacks of books.

Henrietta rolled her eyes. "I'm not saying that you have to – Grandpapa already taught me last summer. I am simply asking that you pretend to have taught me to drive. I'm quite happy for you to be the one with the reins in hand if only you can allow people to think that I have been learning with you."

"The answer is still no. By the by, do you suppose one could actually drive a coach and six through the property?" he asked, looking down from the railings at the shop assistants at their circular desk below.

They were at the Temple of the Muses, a simply glorious bookshop on Finsbury Square that had enjoyed the patronage of Lord Shropshire and his family since it had first opened its doors. The vast building rivalled any ballroom, and Henrietta had no doubt that when the proprietors, Mr Lackington and Mr Allen, had made the boast to which the Duke was referring, they had fully expected to put it to the test.

"Quite likely. In fact, I'm willing to do the honours for you in return for your participation in my little white lie."

Devenish barked out a laugh. "Don't be getting any ideas for pranks into your head. Besides, I wouldn't trust you not to let my horses eat the books."

"At least you aren't afraid I'll scrape the sides of your Phaeton along the bookshelves," she said. "So why will you not pretend to teach me to drive four in hand?"

"My dear girl, you are not listening. If there is so much as a whiff of me hurtling outside of London with you at my side while we are drawn by four of my best horses you will not live down the scandal – and there is a very good chance that I will not, either!"

Henrietta let out an exasperated sigh as Devenish turned his attention to perusing the books. "You've already driven me out three times in your curricle, what possible difference could there be this time?"

"The fact that it would look like an attempted elopement? You're a diamond of the first water, my dear, but I've no desire to be married in such a ramshackle way." He pretended to startle, and turned an overly-horrified gaze upon her. "Good grief, was that your cousin's plan all along? To trick me into marrying her hoydenish cousin and – ouch!"

This last was said laughingly as Henrietta pounded him on the arm with her muff. "Don't be absurd, I've no desire to marry you, and well you know it!"

"Yes, the Mysterious Gentleman still looms large in your heart, does he not?"

Henrietta grimaced. "No, although I daresay it would be comfortable if I could think about him a little less often."

"I suppose if I were forced to elope with you, then you would certainly have bigger problems on your plate than unrequited love. What do you think of this book? Eugenia. Can't say I like the name of it."

Henrietta shook her head, thinking of the lady she knew of the same name. "Lord no, it's dreadful, and your mother will undoubtedly hate it. The heroine wanders around while terrible things happen, then pontificates on them in an utterly sanctimonious fashion. Rather like you are on the matter of pretending to teach me to drive."

"What I don't understand is the need for pretence, since you've already told me you are perfectly capable of driving a chaise-and-four should the need ever arise."

She winced, tapping her foot rapidly in an uneven tattoo as she contemplated how best to phrase her predicament.

"Out with it, Henrietta," said the Duke, not taking his eyes away from the books before him.

"Fine! I may possibly have told someone that you were teaching me to drive after they insulted my skill with the reins."

He glanced over at her. "And why would you choose that particular attack rather than simply taking out your grandfather's curricle to prove your point?"

"Because I was trying to make him feel foolish," she snapped, only just remembering to change the last word from 'jealous'. Nonetheless, she suspected Devenish knew what she had intended to say.

"Well, that was stupid of you," he said, turning his attention back to the books. "What do you think of this one? The Haunting of Widdecombe Abbey. Sounds ghastly so no doubt Mother will adore it."

"I know it was stupid of me, but surely you won't leave me out to dry," she said, chewing on her lip. "All you have to do is pretend."

Devenish placed the book back down. "You are becoming boring, Lady Henrietta. I only agreed to help you become fashionable on the condition you were not boring. Emma assured me that you were intelligent and witty, but she does seem to have quite peculiar notions when it comes to the people that she loves. I mean, she married Loughcroft."

Henrietta bit back down the first ten tart replies she wanted to fling at him, reminding herself forcefully that he still classed as an acquaintance more than a friend. "My apologies, Your Grace, I did not mean to offend."

He looked up from the book he had selected. "Good grief, what was that?"

"An apology," she said through gritted teeth.

"Yes, I know what 'sorry' is. I was rather asking why on earth you thought it was appropriate."

Henrietta frowned, not sure of his point. "I was apologising for boring you. I appreciate the fact that you are doing Emma a favour by helping me cut a dash, and did not mean to whine at you."

Devenish sighed and shook his head. "No, no, no, Lady Henrietta. Never apologise for such matters. The dashing do not say sorry or else the Ton will devour them whole and use their bones as toothpicks. Remember, you are condescending to spend your time on such a poor specimen such as myself, and do not let me forget it."

"But it is you who-" she began, but he held up a hand to stem her argument.

"Are you going to listen to my advice, or not?" he demanded.

Henrietta stared at him for a long moment, her eyes narrowing. "It rather depends on whether this is a trick question."

Devenish laughed. "You are learning – good! Never give anyone an inch, never apologise, and never let them see weakness. You should be pointing out to me what an honour teaching you to drive would be for a poor specimen like myself, rather than trying to wheedle me into doing something as a favour. Which reminds me – don't ask for favours, because you never know when they will be cashed in."

"You have a very different experience with the Ton to me," said Henrietta, shaking her head.

The smile on Devenish's face was not a particularly nice one. "You have no idea. Now, what do you think of this book?"

"A better choice; light-hearted and quite irreverent in the humour. Here, I found these two novels as well; I'm sure the Duchess will love them." She paused just as she placed the books into his hands, their fingertips brushing. "Does this count as a favour?"

Devenish grinned. "I see you are learning. Come, let us go make our purchase downstairs and see if we cannot drive to Gunters for an ice. I'll even let you take the reins if you like."

Henrietta felt the smile tugging at her lips. "You'll let me drive that beautiful pair of yours?"

"Indeed; didn't you say you were taught by your grandfather? Lord Shropshire is a noted whip, even now. If he trusts you to drive his curricle, I am not about to second-guess his opinion."

"But not a chaise-and-four?" she asked, unable to resist.

"No, my dear; as much as I would like to witness you racing through the country with four in hand, I'd rather not be forced to marry you as a result."

"Which doesn't alleviate the fact that I foolishly claimed you were going to teach me to drive," she said, feeling her shoulders droop.

"Have you listened to anything I've said?" Devenish replied, his tone thick with exasperation as they walked down the staircase and toward the circular desk where the booksellers waited. "Turn this to your advantage!"

"I suppose…" said Henrietta, turning the problem over in her mind, "I suppose that you will be letting me drive your phaeton through London, which is quite a feat in and of itself."

"Excellent start," said Devenish, nodding his approval.

"And perhaps… perhaps if you were to witness me driving Grandpapa about in his chaise-and-four, you might feel that there was nothing you could teach me considering I had learned to drive with a master."

"Very good," laughed Devenish, "and that certainly puts me in my place, as well!"

Henrietta grinned and slipped her arm through his. "Thank you, Your Grace. I'm learning so very much about being dashing, and I am quite enjoying it."

"That's because you are dashing, you silly goose," he said, giving her nose a lazy flick. "You only needed to stop hiding."

"It's easy with you," she replied truthfully, and smiled.

He stared at her for a long moment, not speaking, before giving his head a small shake and turning back to the matter at hand.

"Let's buy these books, shall we? Gunters awaits!"

*

When the Marquis of Shropshire arrived at the coachmaker's warehouse in Longacre, everyone went into a flurry, much to his amusement. Although no longer as spry as he had been in his youth, it was heartening to know that the sight of his coat of arms on his carriage door was enough to excite the gentlemen famed for making some of the greatest conveyances in all of England.

"It is so good to see you again, my Lord. I am afraid that my manager is away this afternoon, but I am happy to serve you as best I can," said the salesman, bowing low enough that the Marquis could see the distinctive balding spot at the crown of the young man's head.

"Thank you, Mr Peasbody," replied Lord Shropshire.

Mr Peasbody seemed inordinately flattered by the fact the Marquis remembered him from their previous encounters, possibly unaware of the fact that Lord Shropshire prided himself on remembering the faces and names of people who served him.

"Yes, my Lord, that is my name indeed. It has

been too long since you graced us with your presence. Is the barouche still to your liking?"

The Marquis smiled. "Yes, it is perfectly suitable for the needs of myself and my Lady, as you are no doubt aware since we drive through Hyde Park at the Fashionable Hour often enough. No, my good man, I'm here to purchase something for my Granddaughter."

Mr Peasbody brightened, but with some trepidation in his eyes. The Marquis refused to allow his amusement to show, as he watched the man calculate the likelihood that he truly intended to buy yet another vehicle, or simply out to idle away a few hours.

"We are more than happy to serve Lady Henrietta, of course. And how is she finding the gig that so entranced her the summer before last?"

"It's perfect for her tooling about the estate, but she was hardly going to bring it all the way to London with her," responded Lord Shropshire as he cast his eye over a showy-looking high perch phaeton. "She needs something for when we're in town, or if we venture to Brighton for a few months."

"The high perch is an excellent choice, my Lord. Fashionable and stylish, yet dare I say, too much for the average young miss to handle." He gave a sycophantic smile. "However, having had the privilege of seeing Lady Henrietta take the reins of several vehicles, I would have no such qualms about her capability of handling such a conveyance. Would you like to take it out for a drive?"

The Marquis shook his head. "seems like every other chit intent on cutting a dash drives a high-perch phaeton nowadays – and half of them are overturned within a month of the purchase! No, I don't want my Granddaughter being mistaken for a member of the fast set."

He noted the curricle at the far end of the show-room and made his way over to it, Mr Peasbody chattering at him the entire time. It was equipped with the newer elliptical springs giving it a well-balanced look, and although this particular model was painted the fashionable yellow, an idea took root as the Marquis pictured his daughter tooling about Hyde Park in such a vehicle.

"I think a curricle will suit her tastes very well, although I have a few modifications I would like to make so that she sits a little higher than the rest of the rabble driving around London. And red, not this bumble-bee yellow that everyone loves so much. I want the body of the curricle as deep a red as you can manage, aye with the wheels to match."

"And the hood?"

"Black of course, with seats of red silk edged in black leather." A smile played across Lord Shrop-shire's lips as he contemplated a visit to Tattersalls, and the inevitable hunt for a perfect pair of match chestnuts to complement both the curricle and its new owner.

"How soon can you have it ready?"

"In a matter of weeks at most, my Lord," promised Mr Peasbody, no doubt picturing a large amount of money filling the company coffers – and no doubt his own pocket as well.

Lord Shropshire paused to consider the events already booked into his calendar, as well as Henrietta's desire to take the town by storm as early as possible in the Season.

"Have it to me by the end of the month, and I will add an additional twenty pounds to your payment."

At first, it seemed as though Mr Peasbody would faint dead away, but the small man rallied, and for one horrible moment, Lord Shropshire thought he was going to salute.

"If you would come through to the office, my Lord, I am certain we can get everything underway and delivered to your satisfaction by next Friday."

The Marquis took one last look back at the coach and allowed himself a small smile. He'd have to put a suggestion into his wife's ear that they would need to purchase a cherry-red riding habit for Henrietta, but the overall effect would be worth it.

If Henrietta wanted to cut a dash in town, then she needed to show off her natural skill with horses, both as a rider and driver. And he knew exactly who to rope in to help him.

CHAPTER SIX

Lord and Lady Putney, although perhaps not the most Tonnish of couples, could always be counted on to host a marvellous ball. The stunning chandeliers – Lady Putney's pride and joy – glittered with the flames of hundreds of beeswax candles reflected in the cut glass drops, while additional candelabras graced the otherwise shadowed corners of the ballroom.

Henrietta sat at the side of the room, fanning herself as she chatted amiably with her friends Lady Cordelia and Miss Beatrix Manning. They had all arrived too late to join the current set – a quadrille – so were enjoying a gossip as they reviewed the dresses of various people dancing.

"Do you think Lady Eugenia meant to wear puce tonight?" said Cordy with a grimace. "Surely someone told her that under candlelight it looks quite hideous."

"Considering how superior acts to everyone, I rather suspect she was told the opposite," said Beatrix, smiling at her cousin. "And from the look on Mr Filey's face, it appears her conversation is no more improved than normal."

"Poor Herbert," sighed Henrietta, casting a pitiful smile in that gentleman's direction. "I propose that we all dance with him this evening and be as happy and gay as possible to make up for his ordeal."

"Definitely – but do you mind awfully if I reserve the waltz for someone a little more dashing? Herbert is a dear, but he's not the most romantic of individuals," said Cordy.

"Who did you have in mind?" asked Henrietta.

Cordy looked thoughtful as she looked about the room. "There's Devenish, I suppose, although he's quite besotted with you, so there's little point in angling for an invitation from him."

"He's not besotted in the least!" laughed Henrietta. "He is just amusing himself at the expense of the Ton, and I am quite happy for him to add to my consequence as he does so."

"Is he not teaching you to drive, then?" asked Beatrix, "I heard you were seen tooling about in his carriage when everyone knows he wouldn't trust anyone with his horses."

Henrietta smirked, remembering her argument with Devenish at the Temple of the Muses. "There's nothing for him to teach me, for Grandpapa had me handling horses before I could even walk. His Grace allows me to drive his curricle because he acknowledges that I have an excellent hand."

"She's also modest," said Cordelia, and all three of them laughed.

"Devenish is a good dancer though," said Henrietta. "Almost as good as my cousins Loughcroft and Gloucester. I may be related to them both, but they have excellent form and cannot help but make their partners seem graceful."

"Gloucester isn't here, and besides, both him and Loughcroft are married," said Cordy, dismissing the idea of them with a wave of her hand.

"I wish I knew Lord Loughcroft well enough to dance with him," said Beatrix, ignoring Cordelia's surprise. "Being a Wallflower is quite boring at times, and since he's so monstrously in love with his wife, no one could accuse me of trying to trap him into marriage."

"Are you still angry at Lady Eugenia over that?" asked Cordy. "Because you jolly well should be, as it was hardly your fault that Lord Standish asked you to dance the reel rather than her."

"It doesn't bother me too much," said Beatrix

with a shrug. "She's making a marvellous character in my novel, and will no doubt come to a satisfyingly sticky end."

"How is the novel coming?" asked Henrietta, leaning forward eagerly. "If I pay you a visit tomorrow, will you read the next few chapters to us? I simply must know whether the man she saw in the fog was the villain or the hero!"

"If you really want to," laughed Beatrix. "But only if you promise to take me out driving one day in return."

"Deal," said Henrietta.

"Witnessed and verified," said Cordelia with mock solemnity.

Which only served to cause the three of them to start laughing again.

"Good evening ladies," said Lord Loughcroft as he appeared beside them, "may I hide among your number before the sense of false ennui infecting my fellow members of the Ton causes me to lose the will to live?"

"Of course you may," smiled Henrietta as he took a seat between her and Beatrix. "You know Lady Cordelia and Miss Manning, I believe?"

Loughcroft smiled. "Indeed I have had the pleasure of spending a few minutes in their company on many occasions. How do you both do?"

"Very well, my Lord," replied Beatrix with a smile that Henrietta knew meant that her friend was drinking in every detail of Loughcroft's exquisite clothing.

"Capital! And may I inquire as to the source of such merriment amongst you three?"

"Driving, horses and romance," supplied Cordy, which sent both Henrietta and Beatrix off into peals of laughter.

Loughcroft just nodded knowingly. "The most important things in life, my dears. I once knew a man who lost the love of his life; never seen a fellow so melancholy. Terrible thing."

"The poor dear; did she marry someone else?" asked Beatrix

Loughcroft gave a shout of laughter. "Good grief, no! Well, that would have been something of a scandal, wouldn't it? No, he lost her in a card game. Swore blind that nothing could beat four knaves. Apparently, he forgot about Kings, and his opponent was holding them all. Terrible business, really. He had to pay up, of course, but he was as sick as a dog about it."

Cordy and Beatrix exchanged glances, probably trying to recall if they'd ever heard of anyone so lost to all sense of propriety as to engage in such a card game. Henrietta, used to her cousin's husband by now, just grinned in encouragement.

"My Lord, are you truly telling us that your friend bet the woman he loved on the turn of a card?" said Cordy.

Loughcroft looked taken aback. "My dear Lady, what kind of shabby-genteel rogues do you think I count as my friends?"

Henrietta had to stuff her fist into her mouth to keep from laughing, but Cordy looked torn between horror and intrigue.

"I'm sure I cannot say, my Lord, not knowing you well beyond your reputation as an arbiter of fashion, but you are the one who said your friend lost the love of his life in a card game."

Loughcroft nodded. "Exactly! A beautiful chestnut with perfect bloodlines and long legs. He was devastated when he had to say goodbye; his valet had to carry him back to his library while he sobbed like a child, and they say he didn't eat a thing for weeks. If that weren't bad enough, a month or so later who should he run into at Hyde Park? His opponent and the chestnut, looking happy as a lark as she tossed her head at the world. He took to sitting in a chair by the fireplace at Boodles, staring at his glass for hours on end. I'm telling you, Ladies, love is a terrible business if you lose it."

Henrietta could no longer contain her mirth as understanding dawned on the faces of her friends.

"My Lord… would I be correct in assuming that the love of your friend's life was a horse?" asked Beatrix

Loughcroft rolled his eyes. "Of course it was his horse. Considering the way you brought up a fiancé, I'm deuced concerned about the types of novels you ladies have been reading."

Cordy bristled. "We have excellent taste in novels, my Lord!"

"Doesn't sound that way to me, what with the heroes betting their fiancé's away in card games."

"I've never heard of that happening in a single book that I've read!"

"They why would you think it happens in real life?" asked Loughcroft, looking surprised. "I know you're young, Lady Cordelia, so I'm sure you won't take it amiss when I advise you that you really shouldn't go about accusing men of having ramshackle friends who'd do such a scandalous thing. Very bad Ton."

Cordy opened and closed her mouth without a single sound coming out, while Beatrix looked as though she was committing the entire conversation to memory – no doubt for inclusion in a future novel. As for Henrietta; she didn't care if it was considered vulgar to laugh so hard that tears were forming at the corners of her eyes; the situation was hilarious.

The formation of the next set of dances was called, recalling all four of them to the present. Within moments there were a number of eligible young men bowing to them, most vying for the chance to lead Cordy out in the Cotillion.

Loughcroft turned to her. "Meant to say, Coz, can I have this dance?"

Remembering Beatrix's comment from earlier, Henrietta shook her head.

"I'm afraid I'm already promised for this set," she lied, "but Miss Manning is an excellent dancer, and not yet engaged."

Loughcroft, ever the gentleman, turn to the blushing Beatrix and offered his hand. "Will you take pity on me?"

"I would love to dance with you, my Lord," said Beatrix, looking extremely happy. "It would be an honour."

As Cordy selected her partner, the remaining gentlemen turned toward Henrietta, all smiles as they requested her hand for the dance.

"Really, gentlemen, you can hardly expect a Lady of such quality to pick over another's leftovers," said Devenish as he strolled toward them. With lazy arrogance, he held out his hand. "My fairest Henrietta; will you take pity on such an unfortunate as myself and dance with me?"

Henrietta could barely keep her face straight as she took his hand and rose gracefully to her feet.

"Indeed I will, Your Grace," she said, then bit down on her lip to keep from laughing.

"Keep it together," Devenish murmured. "Remember that you are condescending to be seen with me, not laughing at me."

"I'm not laughing at you," she murmured back. "I had no idea you could be so brazen!"

His lips twitched, but he managed to maintain the façade of an aloof aristocrat. "Are you doubting the sincerity of my actions, or of my words?"

"Both," she shot back. "You are an incorrigible rogue, Your Grace, but also proving to be a good friend. I am glad that we met, and I only hope that you are enjoying this new friendship as much as me."

"I constantly surprise myself with the discovery of just how much I enjoy being in your company," replied Devenish.

Henrietta was surprised at his odd choice of words, but then the music began, and she lost herself in the joy of the cotillion.

*

"Thank you for taking Henrietta shopping last week," said the Marchioness before taking a dainty sip from her champagne flute. "I do think she looks particularly pretty this evening, even if I do say so myself."

Emma smiled, remembering how her younger cousin had attacked the bolts of coloured muslin during their shopping trip before deciding on the pink she was currently wearing.

"It was no trouble, Grandmama, and for all the fun I had I suspect that the modiste enjoyed the session even more," laughed Emma, shaking her head at the memory. "I've never seen her so enthusiastic over a client before – and Henrietta so interested in everything the woman had to say!"

"Henrietta has always had such a good figure and bearing," sighed the Marchioness. "It's been a waste to see her wearing such boring gowns. She's tried so hard to be perfect, instead of realising that her flaws are some of the best things about her."

"Well she's already started to take the advice to heart, and I even found myself coveting her new bonnet," laughed Emma, "and believe me when I say that has never happened before!"

The Marchioness smiled. "It's only been a few

weeks, and I confess that even I have been shocked by the change in her. She seems to be enjoying herself immensely, and I thank the Duke for that."

"I knew Devenish would be good for her," said Emma as she watched them dance. "He's doing a capital job of keeping her entertained without letting her cross the line of good behaviour. She apparently wanted to re-enact Abby's infamous drive down St James', but he yawned and said that dashing young heiresses didn't follow in the footsteps of others, but rather forged a trail of their own."

The Marchioness smiled, although she put down the champagne flute with a little more force than necessary. "I'd like to say that such a prank would amuse me, but I find that where Henrietta is concerned, I am far more forbidding."

Emma shook her head. "There is no need to worry, Grandmama. Devenish won't let her come to any harm, and is doing his very best to scare off the rakes while leaving space for her to interact with suitable gentlemen, like Mr Filey, or Lord Standish."

"Yes, they seem to have taken very well to the real Henrietta, haven't they?" said the Marchioness, not without considerable pride. "There was almost a scuffle at last night's party over who got to escort her into supper!"

"Who won?"

"Devenish, naturally." The Marchioness sighed and shook her head. "It's all nonsense, of course, and although they've stopped writing her poetry, Lord Standish was threatening to serenade her instead, and I have a horrible feeling he will go through with it, just for a lark. I don't believe a single one of them – Henrietta included – think that this is anything but a bit of fun. Not one of them has any intentions toward her or she toward them!"

"Still in love with Cottingham, is she?" said Emma, giving her Grandmother a sympathetic smile.

"Of course she is – and he is with her if the puppy weren't such a fool about it. The two of them have been thick as thieves since their childhood, and although I had hoped for higher than a mere baron, I would happily accept him into the fold if only he'd stop making the girl so miserable."

"Men can be such idiots," sighed Emma. "When I think of the lengths I had to go to with Loughcroft, and you only have to consider how long it took George to realise he was in love with Abby."

"Yes but I don't blame Cottingham too much," said the Marchioness. "At least, I blame him for upsetting Henrietta, but not for taking her for granted. She's been at his beck and call her whole life, just waiting for him to wake up instead of making him see for himself that his perfect mate has been living next door all these years. Why he took it upon himself to advise our girl to start searching for a suitable husband is beyond me."

"By which you mean he's a clod head."

Lady Shropshire sighed. "Yes, a perfectly intelligent, amiable, and well-intentioned clod head."

Emma shook her head. "I shall endeavour to do everything I can to prevent my son being as big a clod head as the males who have preceded him in the Ton."

The Marchioness snorted. "He's male, Emma. Your son will be as idiotic as the rest of his sex, despite your best intentions. Don't you think that Lady Cottingham has done her very best to steer her son toward Henrietta?"

Emma raised her eyebrows in surprise. "Has she really?"

"Of course she has! She gets on perfectly well with Henrietta for a start, and it wouldn't hurt if her future daughter-in-law happened to be richer than Croesus, now would it?"

Emma shuddered. "How mercenary."

"It's a very sensible approach," said her Grandmother with a sniff. "Would you prefer the woman your own boy falls in love with to be penniless or an heiress of great consequence?"

"When you put it like that I suppose I would be

very grateful if he marries for both love and fortune," said Emma as she gave the matter some thought, "but I still think it sounds quite horrid to consider money a pre-requisite for a future mate."

"That's because you've never been poor," said the Marchioness. "But Lady Cottingham is a smart woman, and she knows better than to openly push Henrietta as a choice for a bride."

Emma frowned. "Then how can she help us?"

Her Grandmother smirked, and Emma knew immediately that whatever Lady Cottingham was doing to bring Henrietta and her son together, it was at Lady Shropshire's behest.

"She is introducing him to eligible young ladies," said the Marchioness. "Day and night she is working on it, inviting them to pay calls on her, tasking James with driving her around the park with one or two young misses in tow. She ensures that he has company at every supper, ball and card game they are invited to, and of course only picks the most perfectly respectable, demure debutantes to bring to his attention. If their mothers happen to be vulgar harpies, so much the better."

Emma blinked a few times, watching as her grandmother took another delicate sip of champagne.

"That is absolute genius," she declared. "I wish

I had thought of that myself."

"Remember it for when your own boy is old enough to start courting," said the Marchioness. "Of course, there's a chance that Cottingham might take to one of these insipid young girls – miss Juneberry, for example, is both pretty and intelligent from what I hear, despite having a vulgar mother – but it's a small risk and one worth taking. No, Lady Cottingham is far more concerned about Devenish."

"The Duke? Why on earth would she be worried about him?"

The Marchioness nodded over at him, just as he laughed at something her cousin said. "He seems very taken with Henrietta."

Emma rolled her eyes. "Of course he does, that's the whole point. He's doing his best to help convince the Tonto realise what an absolute diamond my cousin is, and hopefully stir up a little jealousy in Cottingham's chest."

"You aren't worried that he'll fall in love with her? I confess that I would not be disappointed in the match; the boy's reputation has always been far worse than he deserved. And he's a Duke."

Emma considered this for a moment. "It's possible I suppose, but despite Henrietta's protests to the contrary, I strongly suspect that she is so deeply in love with Cottingham that no one else will ever do for her. Besides, it might do Devenish some good to have his heart broken a little. He's so used to being chased and petted he's forgotten that not every woman in the world is desperate for his hand in marriage."

"You are a schemer after my own heart, my dear," said the Marchioness, and Emma found herself blushing with pleasure at the compliment.

The set came to an end, and Devenish led the flushed and laughing Henrietta to their side.

Emma smiled at her young cousin. "It sounds like you're enjoying yourself, my dear."

"Much more than I thought I would! Although since Cordy and Trix are here, that's not unexpected!"

"You wound me," sighed Devenish, and Henrietta gave him a playful punch on the arm that made the Marchioness raise an eyebrow.

"One should not hit a Duke, Henrietta. Or anyone, for that matter, and certainly not at a ball."

Henrietta gave an inelegant shrug. "Then pray tell him not to be so absurd, Grandmama!"

The Marchioness looked at Devenish, somehow managing to keep her face straight. "Do not be absurd, Your Grace, in the presence of my Granddaughter. It leads her to forget that she was raised at Shropshire House rather than in a barn."

"I shall endeavour to be serious," he replied, even as Henrietta giggled.

"I am not in the habit of requesting miracles," said the Marchioness, rather ruining the impact by allowing herself a small smile before taking another sip of her champagne.

"Emma, do you go to the theatre tomorrow?" asked Henrietta as she disengaged from Devenish's arm and dropped into the free seat with all the grace of a goutish elephant.

"I don't know that we have any formal plans, but I'm sure Loughcroft would enjoy a trip to Drury Lane. Is there any particular reason?"

"We are escorting Henrietta and a few of her friends tomorrow evening, so our box shall be the envy of all in attendance," replied Lady Shropshire with an indulgent smile.

"It's Cordy and Trix," explained Henrietta, "and I plan to laugh a great deal with the both of them – but that's by the by. Cordy had a simply marvellous idea on how to cut a dash tomorrow evening, but it is to be a surprise, so you have to be there to witness our triumph."

"Even I am not privy to the secret," sighed Devenish.

"I'm intrigued as to how you intend to cut a dash," said Emma, and she meant every word. "And you are certain that you won't be flying too close to the wind?"

"I've already approved their little scheme," said the Marchioness. "I have to admit it is quite clever of Lady Cordelia."

"And are you to be in the party, Your Grace?" asked Emma, but it was Henrietta who answered.

"Lord no, I don't want people to claim Devenish is dangling after me," replied Henrietta with a laugh so genuine that Emma was reassured she was not at risk of losing her heart to the Duke. Devenish's smile, on the other hand, had a forced quality that surprised her.

"Good God, they'll start to expect me to write you poetry," he said with a shudder.

"Anything but that!" laughed Henrietta. "Besides, he will be escorting his Mama to the theatre, won't you, Devenish? So he will understandably be devoted to her all evening. We promised to visit their box after the first act finishes, for the Duchess has enjoyed a novel I recommended for her and wants to thank me for having better taste in literature than her son."

"It is a very good thing that I have a high opinion of myself," said the Duke to no one in particular, "or else by now I would be quite beside myself."

"So will you be at the theatre tomorrow, Coz?"

asked Henrietta, deliberately ignoring Devenish.

"I wouldn't miss it for the world," declared Emma, although she suspected that it was the drama unfolding off the stage that would doubtless hold her attention the most.

CHAPTER SEVEN

James tried very hard to be gentlemanly about the whole thing and not compare his mother's guests with those of Lord and Lady Shropshire, but it was a nigh on impossible task to achieve.

The Cottingham's box was located on the opposite side of the theatre to that of the Shropshires, and as such he had the perfect view of three lively and very pretty young women as they giggled and laughed their way through the farce.

Lady Cordelia and her cousin, Miss Manning, were a year or two younger than Henry, but they seemed to have forged a solid friendship in the year that he had been away. They made a striking trio, with Henry's guinea-gold hair in contrast to Lady Cordelia's rich black tresses and Miss Manning's luxurious auburn curls.

Whether by accident or design, the three of them were also wearing practically identical gowns and had their hair styled in the exact same fashion. Indeed, they were attracting considerable attention from many other spectators as well, with some men in the pit openly ogling the three of them.

"Are you enjoying the play, my Lord?" said Miss Juneberry, politely, recalling him to his surroundings. Since he hadn't been paying a blind bit of notice to the antics down on the stage, he was unable to form an intelligent reply one way or the other.

Honesty seemed the best policy. "I'm afraid that I've been acting like a gossipy old spinster and ogling the crowd for tidbits of information," he said, hoping his smile conveyed this to be a joke. "It's been so long since I was in London that I'm afraid I will have forgotten what everyone looks like."

Miss Juneberry smiled, but her eyes lingered a moment longer than necessary on the Shropshire's party.

"I thought the purpose of coming to the theatre was more to see and be seen?" he replied, trying to sound teasing, although it appeared that his attempt fell flat.

"It certainly seems that Lady Cordelia is causing a stir tonight," said Miss Juneberry, "but then she is both devastatingly pretty and an heiress to boot."

"I think it's because the three of them look like they are sisters all dressed up the same like that," interjected her mother, nodding appreciatively in their direction. "Doesn't Lord Shropshire look pleased with himself, what with his wife and three beautiful young things in the box with him. No doubt he's reminiscing about the halcyon days of his youth!"

"Yes, he always had been an extraordinarily charming man," said James' mother, "not that anyone has ever come close to the Marchioness in his heart."

"It must be wonderful to be adored like that," said Miss Juneberry in a wistful voice, and James was surprised to see both his own mother and hers sighing in agreement.

Thunderous applause alerted him to the fact that first act had finished, and he jumped up to his feet. "May I escort you for a turn about the hallways, Miss Juneberry?" he asked.

"If Mama does not need me," replied his guest, glancing at her mother and receiving a long, word endorsement of the benefits of walking around with such a fine young gentleman as Lord Cottingham.

"I do hope that you forgive Mama her enthusiasm," said Miss Juneberry once they had exited the box. "I have told her several times that you are quite in love with Lady Henrietta, but she refuses to listen to me on that head."

James tripped, only just managing to save himself from crashing to the floor and dragging the young Lady down with him. "Good grief, in love with Henry? What on earth gave you that impression?"

Miss Juneberry cocked her head to the side, looking for all the world like a young sparrow as she did so. "Are you not? My apologies my Lord, I'm usually very observant about such things."

"No! Of course I'm not in love with Henry," James laughed, although it sounded forced even to his own ears. "I've known her since she was practically a babe in arms."

"No doubt that accounts for why I thought she was in love with you as well, then," replied his companion, which nearly sent him sprawling a second time.

"No, there I must correct you, my dear, for Henry would no doubt roast me for a week if I told her of this conversation. Why she scolded me most horribly only the other week for not reading her letters while I was in Montreal, and that's hardly lover-like behaviour, now is it?"

He couldn't quite name the expression on Miss Juneberry's face, but it was several moments before she seemed able to find the words she was looking for. "I would think, my Lord Cottingham, that if the man I loved had failed to read any of my letters in the year that we were apart, that I would scold him quite horribly upon his return, too."

"I- I had not thought of it quite like that," he said to no one in particular.

"Of course you know Lady Henrietta far better than I do," conceded Miss Juneberry, and he would be damned if she didn't also pat him on the hand as though he was nothing more than a schoolboy. "I'm sure you're quite right, and she sees you as nothing more than a friend from her childhood."

James could not think of anything else to say on the topic, and quickly steered it to inane niceties for the rest of their promenade. Both he and Miss Juneberry took the opportunity to say hello to a number of their acquaintances, which ate up the remaining time together until the first possible moment where James could politely return his companion to their box.

He couldn't help but look up to the Shropshire's box, only to discover that although the Marquis and Marchioness were conversing with some friends that he did not recognise, the three young ladies were nowhere to be seen.

Miss Juneberry patted him on the arm. "They are over there, in His Grace's box with the Duke and his mother."

The ease with which she had understood was

unnerving, and under any other circumstances, he may have liked her considerably. As it was, the few things she uttered to him were either society nothings or lightning quick insights, the latter of which he was debating the accuracy of.

She was, however, correct on the location of Henry and her two friends. The ladies were laughing uproariously and presenting the most charming picture, while the swarthy Duke smiled at them in a way James could only consider as wolfish. The frail-looking woman sat in a low chair beside Devenish could be none other than the Dowager Duchess, who appeared completely entranced by her young visitors, even as her son kept her hand firmly locked within his own.

"It's remarkable to see how dutiful His Grace is to his immobile mother," said the elder Mrs Juneberry to no one in particular, "although his reputation is of course quite terrible when it comes to matters of the heart. I heard Lord Rothman once called him out due to some havey-cavey business with his sister. I do hope that someone has put a word in Lady Henrietta's ear about him."

James was thankful he did not have to respond to the veiled insult, as he felt rather than saw his own mother bristle. "Perhaps you are unaware, Mrs Juneberry, that Lady Henrietta has been a lifelong friend and playmate to my son, and I have long considered her to be a daughter of my heart as much as she was of my poor deceased friend. I assure you if the Marchioness of Shropshire sees nothing contemptible if the Duke's interest in her grand-daughter, then I believe none of the rest of us should, either."

Mrs Juneberry made a flustered apology that was as incoherent as it was sincere, so it was a relief when the actors returned to the stage, and the applause drowned out her rambling.

Miss Juneberry, however, squeezed his hand a second time. When he looked down into her face she smiled and mouthed the word "sorry" , but whether for her earlier comments or for the behaviour of her mother, he was not entirely sure.

*

The Duchess was an absolute delight, thought Henrietta, and she was very pleased that Devenish has asked her and her friends to remain in their box for the next act. His smile, which could only be described as brotherly, had not left his lips since they had entered and begun to engage his mother in conversation.

"So which of you darling girls came up with the idea of matching ensemble's this evening?" asked the Duchess. "It was certainly a stroke of genius – I've never had so much attention at a theatre outing before!"

"It was Cordy's idea," answered Beatrix, but her cousin shook her head.

"On not really; it was part of Trix's story, and I thought it would make such a good joke to do it in real life!"

"Her story?"

Lady Cordelia nodded enthusiastically. "Trix is a writer, you know. She's writing a simply marvellous novel at the moment, and wanted to write a chapter all about the heroine and her friend dressing similar, so that they could confuse the villain."

"Cordy," admonished Miss Manning as her cheeks turned pink. "Please ignore my cousin, Your Grace. It's only some scribbling I do when it's a dull day, nothing of real note."

"Pooh!" said Cordy, making everyone smile. "It's simply wonderful, as are all your stories. Why I'm never as entranced by the novels we bring back from the library as I am by your tales. Don't you agree, Henrietta?"

"Without hesitation," she replied, smiling as Miss Manning flushed an even rosier shade, "and you cannot accuse me of familial affection, either! As to the scene in question, well I was on the edge of the seat waiting to discover if the villain saw through their disguise."

"Which naturally begs the question: if you beautiful ladies are re-enacting the scene from Miss Manning's novel, does that make me the wicked villain?" asked Devenish with a sardonic gaze at the three of them.

"Of course not," said Henrietta as Cordy went off into peals of laughter and Miss Manning looked as though she would die from mortification, "you are simply a background character of no real significance to the plot."

"She wounds me again," cried Devenish, clasping his hands to his chest as though an arrow had pierced his heart.

"It will do that ego of yours some good," said his mother tartly, although her eyes danced with the same merriment that was reflected in those of her son.

"It is a monstrously good story though," said Cordy as she squeezed her cousin's knee.

"I suppose it was too much to suppose that people would confuse us for the same girl considering we all have such different colouring," said Miss Manning, "but I confess I never expected to draw so many eyes to us! I know it's vulgar to say that I'm enjoying the attention, but I'd be lying if I said I was oblivious to it all, or that it was uncomfortable."

The Duchess smiled. "There is nothing vulgar about sharing such confidence among friends. The three of you have garnered so much interest I daresay it will be in all the papers tomorrow, and every young woman worth her salt will be rushing out to purchase matching gowns with her friends."

"How marvellous to be dashing," said Henrietta without thinking, but her friends nodded in agreement.

"And are you hoping to have the book published soon, Miss Manning?" asked Devenish.

Miss Manning shook her head. "No, I keep changing my mind about important events and having to rewrite scores of pages. I daresay it will take me years to get it into a suitable condition."

"She's too embarrassed to send it to anyone," said Cordy, once again causing her cousin to blush.

"Which is such a shame, because I've adored every passage she's read to us, and I think it would be frightfully popular," said Henrietta. She shared a long look with the Duchess, who once again struck her as being a singularly intelligent woman.

"Devenish, what say you we have a small gathering of friends one evening, all amateur poets and novelists alike, and we can share extracts from our work?" said the Duchess. "I myself have that simply dreadful poetry I choose to scribble from time to time, so no one need be worried that their writing will be of a lower quality than my own!"

"I think we should arrange it as soon as possible, but only if Miss Manning promises to attend," said the Duke without hesitation. "Lady Cordelia and Lady Henrietta could be our audience if they do not wish like to write."

"I have a quite terrible story about a Russian prince that I could share," announced Lady Cordelia. "It's awful, and I quickly realised that Beatrix has all the writing talent in the family, but perhaps it will make everyone laugh."

"Is it a comedy?" asked the Duchess.

"Not in the slightest," said Cordy with a cheerful grin, "but when I read it to Beatrix the first time she laughed so hard I feared she'd die from lack of breathing. I shall polish it up so something not utterly contemptible."

"And you, Henrietta?" asked Devenish. "Have you anything to share?"

Her mind strayed to the letters she'd written to James, but lay forgotten somewhere in Canada. "I'm a mediocre writer at best, but I'm sure I could throw something together for the gathering if quality is not a requirement."

"I declare this is going to be one of the best entertainments of the Season!" laughed Cordelia, evidently delighted with the scheme. "You will set a trend, Your Grace, for Literary Gatherings of Dubious Merit."

Thunderous applause drew all of their attention to the stage, where the second act of the play drew to a close.

"Oh dear, and we haven't paid the slightest bit of attention to those poor actors," laughed the Duchess. "Now, off you girls go to rejoin Lord and Lady Shropshire. I shall have my secretary draft up some invitations for the party, and think of who else we can call upon to join in the fun."

Recognising the dismissal as a cover for the fact the Duchess was tired, Henrietta and her friends curtseyed and made their goodbyes. A moment before she exited the box, however, Devenish caught her hand and pressed her fingers to his lips.

"You are a diamond," he murmured. "I haven't seen her so happy for years."

"The theatre is enough to cheer anyone up, and it is impossible to be down when Beatrix and Cordy are in high spirits," she responded.

Devenish laughed, but it was low and throaty and nothing like his normal, slightly mocking amusement.

"You have no idea, do you?" he said, and then shooed her out the box before she could respond.

"I say, I'm very much looking forward to the

Literary Gathering of Dubious Merit," said Cordy, practically bouncing with anticipation.

"What if they hate my novel?" said Beatrix as she shuddered.

"Then we'll know they have no taste," said Henrietta, linking her arm into that of her friend. "No one could hear your story and not think it was quite the cleverest, most amusing tale ever."

"Besides, it will do you good to have to be the centre of attention," said Cordy. "You hide too much as it is."

Beatrix lost all of her nerves as she stood up straight and glared at her younger cousin. "Cordy I'm deliberately dressed in identical clothing to both you and Henrietta in order to be the centre of attention for all the Ton to gaze at."

"But you hide between Henrietta and me."

"That would be the definition of centre."

"Oh hush, both of you," laughed Henrietta, "or you really will bring the attention of the entire Ton upon us! Come, let's get back to Grandmama and Grandpapa before the next act begins!"

"In a moment," said Cordy, looking at someone over Henrietta's shoulder. "I've just seen a friend of mine and – oh, isn't that your neighbour, Lord Cottingham? He's terribly good-looking, isn't he?"

Henrietta just about managed to hide her dismay as she turned to see James approaching them on the arm of that pretty young woman he'd danced with twice at Emma's ball.

"Amelia! I haven't seen you for an age!" cried Cordy as she ran over and embraced the other young woman. "Lady Henrietta, do you remember Miss Juneberry?"

"Yes, we met a few times last Season, I believe," said Henrietta. "How do you do, Miss Juneberry?"

"A pleasure to meet you again, Lady Henrietta," said Miss Juneberry with a pretty curtsey. In fact, everything about her was pretty, from her perfect curls to her flawless skin to her simple gown to her wide, expressive eyes. Henrietta would have been perfectly happy to hate her on principle, were it not for the fact that Cordy, Beatrix and James all seemed to like the girl.

"And to meet you, Miss Juneberry. Are you enjoying the play?"

"Very much so. So much in fact that I believe I am very poor company for Lord Cottingham, as I have barely spoken two words to him this whole evening."

"Nonsense," replied James with an extremely charming smile. "It's an honour to spend the evening with someone who truly enjoys the art of the theatre rather than coming here to see and be seen."

Although the words were not aimed at her, Henrietta felt them like a slap in the face. Staring at the one man she had loved since childhood as he smiled down into the eyes of another woman was bad enough, but to hear him censure her behaviour in such a backhanded way was outside of enough.

"You must forgive us three ladies, then, for there was no other reason for our visit tonight other than to cause a stir," she said as lightly as she could. James turned his attention to her, a brief flash of something she couldn't quite read as he met her gaze.

Cordy, however, seemed completely oblivious to the tension enveloping them.

"Lord, I've never been so happy in all my life as I am this evening," she loudly declared. "What do you think, Amelia? Will all of London be talking about us tomorrow?"

"I think they will be fools not to, for you look monstrously beautiful when you stand together like that, and I confess I've spent the last few minutes memorising the way you've all threaded ribbon through your curls, and intend to copy it forthwith!" Miss Juneberry said, and try as she might Henrietta could not find an ounce of sarcasm or duplicity in the woman's words.

It was so unfair. Not only did James obviously

hold Miss Juneberry in great affection (just look at how protectively he had placed his hand over hers!), she was good-natured, pretty, and apparently intelligent to boot.

The conversation continued around her, with Beatrix and Cordy enthusiastically recapping the evening to their friend, while James smiled benevolently at them and interjected an occasional observation, usually to much merriment.

Henrietta kept the inane smile plastered on her face, laughing when everyone else did, and somehow managing to hold it together when James insisted on escorting the three of them back to her Grandpapa's box, before sauntering off with Miss Juneberry to return to his own.

"Are you quite well, my dear?" murmured Grandmama in her ear just after the third act began. "You look a little piqued."

"I never knew that causing a stir would be so tiring," she replied, trying to force her smile to look genuine.

Grandmama squeezed her hand but said nothing more.

"This has been a deuced entertaining evening," whispered Cordy. "I hope the rest of the Season is as much fun as this, don't you?"

No, thought Henrietta, stealing a glance down

at James' box, even though she knew it would do her heart no good. No, I deuced well hope it's not.

CHAPTER EIGHT

The whirlwind of parties and entertainment that was the Season went into full swing, and Henrietta found herself dragged along into them.

The Duchess's prediction came true, and a rather flattering drawing of herself, Cordy and Beatrix appeared in the London papers titled The Three Graces, which somewhat made up for the more vulgar cartoon, The Three Witches, that Cordy at least found incredibly amusing.

Regardless of any impact that the pictures had on the opinion of the Ton, it could not be denied that Henrietta's new style had catapulted her into a new role as a dashing heiress worthy of the Beau Monde's adoration. Flowers arrive daily, as did invitations to a wide range of events and entertainments.

Although as an heiress and granddaughter to the Marquis of Shropshire she had never wanted for requests for attendance at all the major balls and parties, she suddenly found herself facing five or six options for entertainment each and every evening.

"My word, if I'd known all it took to make you popular was to add a little colour to your wardrobe, I'd have binned those insipid white muslins myself!" Grandpapa had said, laughing at his own joke.

"You wouldn't if you knew the cost of them," Henrietta shot back, which only made him laugh more.

"Hush the pair of you, we have far more important matters at hand," said Grandmama as she sifted through the pile of invitations.

"My dear Lady Shropshire, I think you will find there is nothing more important than the cost of a Lady's wardrobe," said Grandpapa in a perfect imitation of his wife's personal maid.

Henrietta giggled, but her Grandmama chose not to respond, even if her mouth tugged a little way into a smile.

"There's an invitation to dinner with Lady Delby and her girls - I do know how much you like her niece, Beatrix, although I find Lady Cordelia a touch too vivacious for my tastes. Here's an invitation from the Seftons to attend a card party and another from the Sheridans for a Venetian Breakfast. You've a choice of three gentlemen to convey you to the Opera, although I cannot think why when our own box is vastly superior, or of course, there is the Fitzburgh ball which will no doubt be enjoyable, despite the fact I am quite certain that Lady Fitzburgh waters the champagne."

Henrietta couldn't help the grin spreading across her face. Being dashing was proving to be much more entertaining than she'd hoped. "Could we start with the Sheridan's Venetian Breakfast, visit the Opera with whoever is the most interesting company, and then finish up by attending the latter half of the Sefton's card party?"

The Marchioness looked up, her face the picture of surprise. "I know you are enjoying being the toast of the Season, my love, but isn't that a little excessive?"

"I thought dropping in for but half an hour was the fashionable thing to do?"

"If you are Prinny or Brummell I suppose, but it wouldn't be good to have a reputation as flighty."

Henrietta lay back into her chair, throwing one arm across her eyes as she attempted to look dramatic. "I am an heiress, Grandmama. And at least as interesting as Brummell."

Grandpapa looked up from his book with a fond

smile. "You are undoubtedly the second most interesting woman in any room, dear heart, with only your Grandmother to surpass you in beauty and wit."

"Behave, Shropshire," admonished her grandmother, but whether she was conscious of it or not, she preened a little.

"It is a fair assertion, my love. The two of you have been gallivanting about town nonstop for the last three weeks, and our lovely granddaughter is finally taking the town by storm the way you predicted she would on her sixteenth birthday." He nodded towards Henrietta. "Quite frankly, my dear, it is a joy to see you blossoming into the young woman we have always known you to be. I am simply surprised that your grandmother is still determined to attend every party of the Season, and try to take the shine out of you in the process."

"That's because Grandmama is both indestructible and irreplaceable," said Henrietta, and then blew a kiss to the Marchioness.

"While you are both incorrigible," declared Grandmama, but a smile played across her lips. "Never let it be said that I have let age mar my enjoyment of life, but even I know that there comes a point where quality is more important than quantity. In fact, should we consider a small, intimate party here instead? Perhaps invite a few of your friends, like Devenish and Cottingham?"

Henrietta went to say yes, but then the memory miss Juneberry clutching his arm caused the very joy to seep from her body. She didn't want to lose their friendship, but her hopes that he would suddenly wake up and see her as a prospective bride had been put to rest, and she wasn't quite sure how to move forward.

Her grandmother was looking at her oddly, and was no doubt intending to question her hesitation when the door was opened wide, and the Duke announced. Henrietta had never been so glad to see him and practically jumped out of the chair with glee.

"Devenish! I haven't seen you since the theatre!" she cried, holding out her hands to him. He seemed surprised but happy at her greeting.

"Hello to you as well, Lady Henrietta; had I known I would be welcomed with such enthusiasm I would not have let three days pass without calling on you."

"Your Grace, what perfect timing," said Grand-mama, waving the pile of invitations in his general direction. "We are struggling to decide which event to go to next Wednesday."

"Lady Fitzburgh's ball of course," replied Devenish. "I'm surprised you would consider any other option."

"We have it on good authority that she waters down the champagne," said Henrietta in a stage whisper, causing Grandpapa to laugh.

"I agree it is a serious mark against attendance," said Devenish with mock solemnity, "but it is to be a masquerade, and where else would a dashing heiress choose to go?"

Henrietta turned her wide eyes toward Grandmama "You never mentioned that it was a masquerade!"

The Marchioness dug back through the pile of letters to retrieve the invitation from Lady Fitzburgh. "I don't remember – ah yes, there it is, scrawled across the bottom of the invitation in a perfectly forgettable location. It will be quite her own fault if only half the Ton turns up in costume. Honestly, I know she is a peer of the realm, but she really is rather shabby when it comes to entertaining."

"A fair point, Lady Shropshire," said Devenish, struggling to hide his smile. "I think it is only fair to lend a little class to her event, don't you think? If not for the sake of the Viscountess, then for those poor daughters of hers?"

"I do feel sorry for those girls sometimes," sighed Grandmama. "Such taking things, but their mother is a harpy."

"Then it is settled," said Henrietta as decisively as she dared. "We will spend the evening at the Masquerade, and I shall protect you, Your Grace, from the encroaching machinations of Lady Fitzburgh."

"I shall refuse to dance with anyone but you," he replied, and she rolled her eyes.

"At this rate, people are going to start expecting you to propose to me."

"I, for one, am in hourly anticipation of it," added Grandpapa without looking up from his book, which was just as well considering the look of pure horror on the Duke's face.

"Foolish children, all of you," said Grandmama, shaking her head. "I shall accept the invitation from Lady Fitzburgh – on the condition, Devenish, that this is not one of your tricks and you will indeed be there as well. Good Lord, that woman will faint dead away when she receives your acceptance."

"I sent it not three days ago, so I trust she will have recovered by now," said Devenish, before turning to Henrietta. "I came to beg your company this afternoon on a short shopping expedition."

"Thank you for the offer, but since Emma helped trick me out I do not think I have any need to buy so much as a hatpin for the rest of the season," replied Henrietta with a careless shrug. The size and cost of her new wardrobe was quite revolting when she thought about it, and she was rather glad that she was lucky enough to be the granddaughter of one of the wealthiest peers in England and a considerable heiress in her own right.

Devenish, however, tsked loudly at her.

"Firstly, shopping is never finished; one never knows when fashion will change, and you will be in need of a thousand yards of pink lace – don't laugh, it is quite possible. Secondly, I rather meant that I will be the one shopping, and I could do with a lady's discerning eye. It is all Loughcroft's fault, of course. I discovered last night that he has a far more exquisite range of snuffboxes than I currently own, and this must be rectified immediately."

"It would probably be easier to steal all of Loughcroft's snuffboxes," remarked Grandpapa, which made Devenish grin.

"I considered it, but beyond the practicalities of the undertaking he would likely know that I was the thief and set Emma on me, and I am man enough to admit that I am terrified of her."

"That explains so much," said Henrietta, shaking her head at his absurdity. "I shall run upstairs to put on my pelisse and bonnet; I shan't be a moment."

Of course, it took closer to half an hour for Henrietta to prepare for the excursion, but it was obvious upon her return to the sitting room that her absence had not been noted. The conversation she walked into was a pleasant one, and ended with a pointed reminder from her Grandpapa that Devenish must not keep her out for more than two hours.

"Honestly, it's as though they think I'll collapse from exhaustion if I have to walk for more than twenty minutes," she said with a shake of her head once they were safely out on the street.

"It's just their way of showing their love and affection," Devenish replied.

"Yes I know, and losing my father and my aunt so young has made them over-solicitous when it comes to Emma, George and me. Especially me, I suppose, since they've had charge of me since I was nothing more than a babe in arms."

"Do they smother you, then?"

Henrietta shook her head. "No not as a general rule – in fact, Grandpapa was always the one likely to egg me on to do something quite harebrained, like the time I climbed the oak tree, or when I jumped into the lake in the middle of winter. It's this last year that they've fussed over me much more."

"Have you given them a reason to worry?"

"I don't think so," she said after a short pause.

"I suppose I did mope quite a bit when Ja- when my friend went away, but I'm quite recovered now."

Devenish gave one of his enigmatic smiles. "I see," he said, and once again Henrietta was left with the feeling that he could see far more than she wanted him to.

"How is your mother?" she asked in a bid to steer the conversation into safer waters. "Was her invitation to a literary evening genuine, for I wouldn't miss it for the world."

Devenish accepted the change of course without so much as a blink and began to fill her in on his mother's enthusiastic plans for the Literary Gathering of Dubious Merit.

It was a short walk from Hanover Square to the Western Exchange on Bond Street, and as they slipped into an easy conversation, Henrietta was very pleased to note that she was seen upon the arm of the Duke of Devenish by many celebrated gossips, including Lady Jersey and Lady Harden. This latter Lady was some distant relative of Emma's, but after a recent falling out over her daughter, the new Mrs Rowlands, she was quick to spread gossip about anyone connected to Lord and Lady Loughcroft.

Which, in the scheme of things, was quite thrilling.

"Do you know, Your Grace, I've a feeling that being seen with you so often is rendering me notorious."

"Already? It's only been a month; usually it takes at least seven weeks before I raise expectations in the hearts of the gossipmongers. I must have more influence over the Ton than I thought. I do hope Mr Brummell is not too put out by this turn of events, for now that I hold the crown of Chief Arbiter of Fashion and Good Taste, I do not intend to relinquish it."

She rolled her eyes, their friendship established enough for her to know it was impossible to get him to be serious about such things.

In truth, he really was almost as important as Brummell in the world of good Ton. His taste was always impeccable, and a young woman determined to cut a dash could do worse than be guided by his advice regarding clothing and deportment.

Yet no matter how well behaved he was since the end of his self-imposed exile from London, the Beau Monde continued to eye him with a sort of awed suspicion. They copied his style and flattered him due to his ducal status – a Duke of marriageable age would always be welcomed by the Ton, of course - but even the most ambitious of matchmaking mamas would discourage their daughters from setting their caps at him.

Henrietta considered this for a moment. To be fair, that might be because he danced attendance on her in the most shocking way, with Lady Cordelia and Miss Manning the only other young women he paid attention to.

This thought naturally led to those of her current suitors, and she sighed. "Being dashing is not at all what I envisaged."

He glanced down at her with a quizzical smile. "Do you miss being a demure young maid?"

She gave a theatrical shudder. "Lord, no. I hated every moment of being an insipid miss, and feigning a fashionable air of ennui was excruciating."

"But being courted and petted and flattered by the Great & the Good does not fill you with happiness either, I take it?"

She grimaced as she tried to untangle her thoughts to a point where they would be coherent.

"I would be lying if I said that it isn't nice to have my opinion sought out on matters of taste, or being able to show enthusiasm for something rather than pretending to be bored. Plus, I don't think there's a girl in London who would complain about a dance card full of the names of dashing young blades from across the peerage rather than that of stuffy gentlemen who think that women are worth no more than their dowry."

"So what is missing from the dashing Lady Henrietta's life?" he asked.

She thought of James, and then shook her head to banish him.

"A good match, I suppose. It's all very well being the toast of London, but it would be nice to have a gentleman to share all of this excitement within a partnership. That's what I envy in my grandparents' marriage. It may have been a dynastic contract of convenience when they met, but there's no doubt that they love each other very much."

"Like your cousins?"

"Yes," she replied with enthusiasm, always glad to find his thoughts to be in line with her own, "exactly like the Loughcrofts and the Gloucesters. Don't you think it must be the most wonderful feeling in the world to love someone and to have them love you back with equal fervour?"

He took a long time to answer, no doubt thinking that she sounded very young and silly.

"Yes, I think it would be a wonderful thing, indeed. Ah, here we are my dear Lady Henrietta: I beg you to put all your attention to the task at hand, and help me choose a selection of snuffboxes to outshine those of Lord Loughcroft!"

Henrietta smiled and agreed readily to the task, a little embarrassed at her confession and hoping that it did not lead him to think ill of her.

Luckily her fears appeared to be unfounded.

They spent an agreeable hour visiting various jewellers and merchants in order to track down the essential snuff boxes, but it wasn't long before they began a competition over who could find the most vulgar or ugly piece to add to Devenish's collection.

They were still laughing about an absolutely hideous peach-enamelled box covered with gaudy paste jewels that Devenish had insisted on purchasing as they turned back into Hanover Square, and Henrietta gave a little gasp.

Outside of her grandparent's mansion was the most ravishing curricle she has ever seen. The chassis and wheels were a spectacular shade of cherry red, while the hood and seats were of a black leather the shade of a moonless night. The perfect chestnut pair that drew the curricle were no less wondrous, for not only were they two of the most handsome horses she had ever laid eyes upon they were so alike that she could swear they were twins.

"I am in love, and shall marry immediately whoever owns such a setup," she declared. Her Grandpapa's groom, who was holding the reins, grinned at her.

"I cannot allow you to do so, my dear," sighed Devenish, "for I am very much afraid I would fight you for the right to stand at the altar. I have never seen such a perfect match pair in all my days."

"Shall we go inside and see who is visiting?" said

Henrietta, turning toward the house even as she spoke. "I have a marriage proposal to make."

"As do I," laughed Devenish, as the front door opened and Lord Cottingham stepped outside, accompanied by Grandpapa.

"James!" she said, aware from the pained look on her old friend's face that she had not hidden her dismay. "Is this your curricle?"

"I'm afraid not, nor was it here when I arrived a few moments ago, or else I might have been forced to steal it," he said with a false smile. "Have you worked out how to sneak it away without the owner seeing yet, Henry?"

Following his lead, she gave a bright, brittle smile of her own. "I had rather thought to offer my hand in marriage to the owner, but I suspect thievery would be more efficient. His Grace would most likely wrest it from me at the first opportunity, however, so I do not think I would get far in my life of crime."

"I'm afraid marrying the owner is out of the question my dear," said Grandpapa, the banter evidently amusing him greatly. "Now I must pull you away from this little piece of heaven and ask you to step into the front parlour, where a far more interesting mystery awaits. You may as well come too, Devenish, and you Cottingham."

Intrigued, the three of them followed her grandfather, much like puppies promised a bone. In the front parlour, her Grandmama awaited them, a pretty bandbox on the table before her.

"What's this?" asked Henrietta, much to the amusement of her grandparents.

"Open it, my love, and then we shall all know," replied Grandmama with a fond glance at her husband.

Her heart racing for some unfathomable reason, Henrietta removed the lid and pulled back the paper to reveal a cherry red riding habit trimmed with black frogging, and a matching cap. The quality was exceptional, and it was the type of garment designed to be seen and envied.

Her hands shook as she removed it from the box, and she gazed up at her Grandpapa with churning emotion.

"This is so beautiful; does this mean... is the curricle... oh my, am I being an utter brat by hoping...?"

Her grandfather smiled fondly. "That rather depends on if you are hoping the curricle outside belongs to a Lady Henrietta."

"You are the best of Grandpapas!" she half screamed as she launched herself into his waiting arms. He laughed and kissed her head before releasing her long enough to fall into her Grandmama's embrace and thank her just as profusely.

"Can you believe that the carriage and horses are mine?" she said, turning to both Devenish and James. "I'll be the envy of all London once I'm seen driving it!"

"Indeed, and I shall try very hard not to steal them if you take me out for a drive immediately," said Devenish.

At the exact same moment, James said: "Take pity on this envious creature and take me for a turn about the park at once."

There was an awkward pause.

"Oh. Yes. Well, of course I'll take you both out with me for a drive, only it's a curricle so I can hardly take you together, or there will be no room for me," she said, half-laughing at her own poor joke before another, even more awkward silence fell. James and Devenish were looking at each other in a way that could only be considered hostile.

They must both really like those horses, she thought.

"I am afraid that as her Grandfather, I must insist that her first drive out is with me," said Grandpapa, coming to her rescue. She threw him a grateful smile.

"Yes, naturally, I will need to assure him that I haven't rusted my skills with a pair, or that I won't hunt the squirrel at the first opportunity." She glanced toward Devenish and smiled. "Perhaps when we take our drive tomorrow, I can take you out in my curricle rather than the other way around."

"A pleasure," said Devenish, inclining his head.

She glanced at James and her smile faltered. "I'm sure we can find some time to ride out together in the next week or so if you would like?"

"If you can find time to slip me into your schedule, I would be most grateful," he replied, with only a hint of sarcasm tinging his words. "I am sure that you must be dying to change into that riding habit and take your new curricle out for a spin, so I shall bid you adieu."

He bowed and then began to stride out of the room.

"James!" she cried out, causing him to pause. "I, well, that is, are you to attend the Fitzburgh's Masquerade on Wednesday? Only we haven't danced together for an age, and I thought maybe you would like to waltz with me?"

For a long moment she thought he would refuse, but eventually, he glanced over his shoulder and gave a brief nod. "I should like that."

"Go up and change now," urged her grandmother, practically pushing her out of the room. "It will not do to keep those horses standing for much longer."

With barely time to throw a farewell toward Devenish, Henrietta found herself running up the staircase to her bedroom, clutching the red habit to her chest.

What had she been thinking, inviting James to dance with her in such a way! She'd left him no way of politely refusing, and no doubt he wished her at Jericho right now.

She sighed, knowing there was nothing to be done about it now. She glanced down at the riding habit, at the striking shade of red, and a thought occurred to her.

Henrietta smiled. Perhaps James had not wanted to dance with her, but he could not be avoided forever. If he did not want to marry her, there was nothing she could do about the situation.

But at least she could make him regret it just a little.

*

The Marquis allowed himself an indulgent smile as Henrietta drove them about the park with all the grace and skill he had drummed into her since childhood. The sheer joy on her face as she took a corner with precision warmed his heart, although he was aware of a pang of regret that his son was no longer alive to see what a capital horsewoman - what a capital young Lady - she had grown to be.

"I so sorry Grandpapa," she said in a mournful tone, her eyes never leaving the road before them.

"Whatever for, child?"

She glanced at him, a mischievous grin plastered on her face. "For having the best carriage and horses in your stable! This darling gift from you puts everything else in the shade - even Cassidus!"

"Hoyden," he replied, and she gave such a happy laugh he would have willingly bought her another six curricles in each shade of the rainbow.

Although it was not yet the fashionable hour, there were enough people of note in Hyde Park for Henrietta's new coach and horses to be much remarked upon, but not so many carriages that she was unable to show to advantage. The riding habit he felt was a particularly fine touch as it would also help her stand out when riding her filly Iris, and he did not doubt that she would soon be a noted figure in the park that people would look for during their promenades.

"You didn't have to buy me such an extravagant gift, you know," said Henrietta.

The Marquis smiled. "Well, in that case, I will send it back, although I may keep the horses for myself."

"Never in your life!" she replied cheerfully. "You know full well I am only being polite, and in fact have realised how terribly hard done by I have been to not have such a set up much sooner!"

"There's my girl," he laughed and patted her on the knee. "Besides, this is as much for my benefit as yours, for now your Grandmama need not harangue me to escort her on her various morning calls, as it will be far more fashionable for her to tool about with you."

"It's a small price, and one I will pay willingly. Wherever did you find such a perfect pair?"

"That, my dear, remains a secret. I have no wish for Devenish, or Cottingham for that matter, to learn where I acquire my horses."

"As if I'd tell either of them!" Henrietta exclaimed.

"One can never be too careful," replied the Marquis, deciding now was not the time to press the point. "Ah, I believe I see some of my friends riding towards us. Do pull up, my dear."

Henrietta did as she was bid, and moments later the two riders came alongside them. Sir John Lade and his wife, Letitia, were perhaps not the best Ton, but they were firmly in the prince's circle, and as mad about horses as any member of his own family.

"How much for the chestnuts, Shropshire?" said Sir John without preamble. "Name your price."

"Not for sale, my old friend, and even if they were, I'd want nothing less than the pick of your own stables."

Sir John grinned. "Still bitter about losing out on Medley, eh?"

"Not in the least," lied the Marquis. "Besides, these are not my horses, but belong to my granddaughter."

"Lady Henrietta, isn't it?" said Sir John, inclining his head to her. "I remember the time you stole your friend's gig and tooled it about the countryside for a dare. Shropshire bragged about it for weeks."

Henrietta blushed but kept her chin high. "Well he never should have claimed a girl was incapable of taking the corner into the village at anything more than a sedate trot, now should he?"

Both Sir John and his wife laughed heartily.

"Damned if I don't like a girl with spirit," said Lady Lade. The Marquis winced; although he was used to Letitia's frequent swearing, it wasn't something he wanted his granddaughter to adopt as part of her quest to be dashing.

"Thank you," said Henrietta, "that means a lot coming from a noted whip like yourself, Lady Lade."

"And every word meant!" said Lady Lade. "Now, how much for those horses? I simply won't take no for an answer, my dear girl. If my Sir John wants them, then have them we must!"

Henrietta, the Marquis was proud to note, was made of stern stuff. "As much as it pains me to disappoint you both, I'm afraid that I must decline all offers for my chestnuts. When you consider that not only are they beautiful steppers but that they also accessorise quite perfectly with my carriage and habit, you can surely understand that it would be impossible to part with them."

Sir John laughed as though this was the most glorious joke he had ever heard. "Good on you, my girl, good on you! Although I demand that you will come to me first should you decide the breed them."

"Of course – so long as my Grandpapa and His Grace have already declined," replied Henrietta, which sent Lady Lade off into whoops of laughter.

"Lady Henrietta, I had no idea that you were such a spirited filly," said Sir John, which the Marquis took as a compliment.

"Consider the stable, and it is no surprise," he said, smiling indulgently down at her. "She's the pride of our bloodline – although never tell Lady Loughcroft or Lord Gloucester that I said so!"

"I have to say that I'm damned jealous of this

curricle as well," said Lady Lade, eyeing it appreciatively. "Built for speed and precision, from the looks of the thing."

"Ah, but can she back the rear wheels over a sixpence?" asked Sir John with a grin.

"I'm sure that I'm not such an accomplished driver as yourself so I will not be laying odds on that particular endeavour anytime soon," said Henrietta with a perfectly charming smile. "I am afraid I cannot say how well the curricle will perform with the horses set to, Lady Lade, for this is my first time driving this beautiful carriage, and I doubt London will afford me the opportunity to put this rig through its paces."

"Then may I offer my services, Lady Henrietta?" said Letitia with a perfectly charming smile. "Knowing your grandfather I do not doubt you are a nonpareil, but before I insist that Sir John buy me an identical curricle – although naturally in blue, so as to show the greys to advantage! – I simply must discover if it is fit for Helios himself!"

Henrietta glanced at him for guidance. The Marquis smiled and pinched her cheek. "Well as my bones are too old to be driving around as though the devil himself were chasing me, I can think of no woman who I would trust more at your side in a curricle than Lady Lade."

"Good God, Shropshire, was that a compliment?"

laughed Letitia. "Wait until I tell Prinny!"

"For all your faults, Letty – and I hope I am gentleman enough not to list them all in the presence of my granddaughter – I have never doubted your skill with a whip."

"Served with your own sauce, my dear!" laughed Sir John. "We shall call on you soon, Lady Henrietta, and put our heads together to see how best to put you through your paces. Would that be agreeable?"

"What do you say, dearest?" the Marquis asked Henrietta with an encouraging smile.

She took the hint and favoured Sir John and Lady Lade with a beautiful smile. "I look forward to it very much."

"Then it is settled!" declared Lady Lade, inclining her head toward them both. "We shall bid you adieu until next Saturday."

It was not until the Lades were almost out of sight that Henrietta seemed to find her voice.

"Grandpapa, did I really just agree to drive out with Lady Lade?"

"At speed," he replied.

Henrietta blinked a few times. "Good grief, I must be mad! What if she finds me nothing more than a cow-handed whipster? How will I ever hold up my head again?"

The Marquis squeezed her hand. "Now my girl, do you doubt my teaching so much?"

"Never!"

"Then allow me to reassure you on this head. The Lades may not always be considered the best Ton, but they move in exalted circles and have the ear of the fashionable set. When they are witness to your skill with the ribbons, it will be about town within hours that you are a regular nonpareil."

She chewed her lip. "I think, perhaps, everyone would then be forced to see me as a capital horse-woman if I win Sir John and Lady Lade's approval; would you agree Grandpapa?"

In another woman, the statement may have come across as arrogant, but the slight tremor in his granddaughter's voice betrayed her secrets to him.

"You are a capital horsewoman no matter what, my darling, but yes, for all those people who wouldn't know the rear of a horse from its head, Lady Lade's approval would no doubt convince them that you were as talented as Astley's equestriennes."

"Thank you," she murmured, and then gave herself a little shake. "I've kept these beauties standing for too long; shall we drive?"

"Yes, my dear girl. Drive we shall."

CHAPTER NINE

James resisted the urge to pull at his cravat as he ascended the steps to the Shropshire's mansion two at a time. An uncomfortable evening's sleep had brought home to him that he had not behaved in a particularly honourable way the day before, and he was surprised that he would act like a sulky schoolboy over something as silly as having Henry of all people drive him around the park.

There was only the smallest feeling of worry that he might not be welcome at a house where he had run tame since childhood, but the door was held wide, and the butler greeted him with his usual formality, albeit laced with a touch of warmth.

"The family is receiving in the front salon," the butler informed him as he took James' hat and gloves. "There is a small party formed, several gentlemen having chosen to remain for over half an hour, despite the arrival of other guests."

James grinned. "Lady Henrietta's admirers?"

"Amongst others," replied the butler. "Allow me to announce you."

It seemed that the butler had understated the sheer number of people in the Shropshire's salon, which would more accurately be described as a squeeze. Ages ranged from the Marquis himself down to a young girl who looked barely old enough to be out of the schoolroom. They had grouped themselves loosely by age and association, with Henry sat right at the centre, as though everyone else were mere planets in orbit about her sun.

It struck James once again that Henry had altered significantly since his return from Canada - perhaps from before that - but to be completely honest, he couldn't quite work out what had changed.

There was her clothing, of course. Not that James really understood such matters, but even he could tell that her ensembles suddenly included more colour and that there was something more becoming in her general appearance. He'd always thought her a pretty girl, but judging by the number of men vying for her attention, it seemed that the Ton had woken up to this fact as well.

"James!" she said with a smile as he was announced. "How good of you to come, although whether you can find a chair remains to be seen!"

"I'd have arrived at dawn had I known it was the only way to get you to myself for five minutes," he joked and was rewarded with a smile.

"Yes, it's a sad crush, isn't it? I believe everyone saw me driving out with Grandpapa yesterday, and are now being kind to me in order to beg a seat!"

The gentlemen within hearing protested loudly - although a few did take the opportunity to request she take them out for a drive in the coming weeks.

James shook his head but smiled as he did so. In previous seasons when he'd called on the Marchioness and Henry there had usually been a few other visitors, including whichever prosy old bore was trying to capture Henry's hand at the time. It had been something of a joke, for she was always so happy at his arrival if only to escape the attentions of her earnest but dreadful suitor.

"Cottingham, good to see you," smiled the Duke, lounging in the chair beside Henry's as though he was her cicisbeo.

"Your Grace," said James as he bowed, unable to keep some of the ice from his voice. Devenish may have been a Duke, but James had asked around about the man, and although the nickname Devilish seemed a little severe, there was no doubt that the man could be decidedly dangerous to a woman's reputation when he chose to be. Indeed, the odds in Waite's betting book for him either marrying Henry or forgetting she existed by the end of the Season were currently dead even.

Henry was his oldest friend. Although he could hardly reprimand the Marchioness for allowing Devenish such a monopoly on Henry's time, he could certainly watch over her.

"What good luck you chose to come today," said Henry, taking him by the arm and steering him toward a group currently sat at the window. "See, here is Lady Cordelia, Miss Manning, and of course, Miss Juneberry needs no introduction."

"Your servant, ladies," he said, confounded as to why Henry seemed to be smiling with false brightness. "And to you, gentlemen."

This last was directed to several of his friends who returned his greeting with lazy affability.

"We were just discussing His Grace's upcoming Literary Gathering of Dubious Merit," said Lady Cordelia with a welcoming smile. "I do hope we don't drive the Duchess to distraction! Lord Standish is considering reading out his poetry, and I shudder to think how any of us can overcome that."

"It is my lot in life to be a genius of course," said William, much to the laughter of those present.

"And what are you going to read, Lord Cottingham?" asked Miss Juneberry in her usual soft voice.

He favoured her with a smile. "I'm afraid that it's not something I feel I can contribute to," he said.

"Pooh!" laughed Lady Cordelia. "Nothing can possibly be worse than my play! I intended it to be a deeply moving tragedy, but Beatrix laughed so hard when I read the opening lines to them that I was quite put out."

"In her defence, I did the same thing when she read it to me," said Henry. "I thought it was meant to be a comedy and was only being supportive."

"So you see, Lord Cottingham, you have no excuse not to participate," said Lady Cordelia, pretending to ignore her friend. "Indeed, I will take it as a monstrous slight if you do not accept the invitation!"

James was at a loss as to how best respond, considering that he never had received an invitation in the first place. He was, therefore, surprised that his saviour from the predicament ended up appearing in the form of Devenish himself.

"It seems you have no choice but to attend the Literary Gathering of Dubious Merit after all," said His Grace as he joined their group. "You will be forced to contribute some writing of your own, of course, but as you can see, we've set the bar fairly low regarding quality."

"How rude!" said Lady Cordelia, but her eyes were laughing.

"Oh, do come," said Miss Juneberry, smiling up at him. "I'm sure it will be ever so entertaining, and even if none of us can contribute much of worth, Beatrix will be reading from her novel, which will make it all worthwhile."

He saw the appeal behind her words and immediately understood that she must be terrified at the idea of being invited to a semi-private gathering of peers.

No doubt her mother would be scheming to make her the next Duchess of Devenish, poor girl. During their acquaintance, he had learned she was both intelligent and kind but was not exactly noteworthy when seated beside Lady Cordelia and Henry - or even Miss Manning, when it came to it.

He had no intentions toward her of his own, of course, but at least if he were present, then her mother would keep her focus on him rather than trying to bring her daughter to the attention of the Duke.

"Only if Miss Juneberry reads my work first, for I don't want to make a complete cake of myself."

His pronouncement was met with cheers from his friends. He glanced at Henry, knowing she at least would appreciate the heroism he was showing toward Miss Juneberry but found she was not looking at him at all.

"Pray excuse me, Grandpapa wants to tell me something," she said before leaving their group. Devenish, apparently bored now Henry was not among their number, wandered back to his seat without a word, and everyone resumed their original conversations.

"That was not well done," murmured Miss Juneberry as he sat down beside her.

"What wasn't?" he asked in genuine confusion. "I thought you wanted me to join you at the Duke's gathering?"

"I wanted you to join the gathering, not join me at the gathering," she said with an exasperated sigh. "Honestly, men can be so obtuse sometimes!"

"I'm afraid I don't follow," he said slowly, the horrid suspicion that she might be touched in the works occurring to him.

"No, I suppose not. What do you intend to read out?"

The abrupt change of topic made him blink. "I haven't exactly had any time to give it some thought."

"You have two days," she told him. "Will you allow me to make a suggestion?"

"Of course."

"You will read your letters, and then write a reply," said Miss Juneberry, nodding as though this gave her satisfaction.

Before he had a chance to reply, there was a little shout of delight from Henry, who then clapped her hands to get everyone's attention.

"Grandpapa has proposed the most wonderful excursion," she announced, her whole body animated. "We are to drive and ride out to our villa at Merton this coming Saturday, where we will all be served the most delightful luncheon. I know I'm absolutely aching to take my curricle out for a spin - would anyone care to join us?"

There were many shouts of agreement, even from those old enough to know better since Henry's enthusiasm was so infectious, but it was Herbert Filey who asked the question James had been close to voicing himself.

"But who will you care to take up beside you, my dear Lady Henrietta? Are we to fight for the honour? Shall it be pistols at dawn?"

"How unfair!" declared Lady Cordelia loudly. "How am I or Trix or Amelia to try for a place if that is how it will be agreed - or Lady Lade, or the Marchioness for that matter?"

"The Marquis will be driving me down in his

barouche," said Lady Shropshire, "so you may omit us both from the competition."

"And I've already made Lady Henrietta promise to carry me back to London after the luncheon, so I'm out as well," said Lady Lade.

"Shall we toss a coin?" asked William, but he was quickly shouted down.

"I'll not risk a chance at driving with Lady Henrietta to a lucky throw," said Herbert. "What we need is a game of skill."

"In which case, may I suggest jackstraws?" said Devenish.

James blinked a few times, wondering if he had misheard. "I'm sorry, Your Grace, but did you just suggest we play at jackstraws to decide?"

"How perfect!" said Lady Cordelia, and everyone quickly voiced their agreement.

"Only if I get to play as well," said Henry. "It seems monstrous unfair that I should miss out on the fun!"

"But who will you take up beside you should you win?" asked Miss Manning.

"Why, whoever I choose to."

"I believe that is perfectly fair," declared William Standish, "and have I mentioned just what a wonderful, talented, beautiful driver you are, Lady Henrietta?"

"There's little point trying to turn me up sweet," laughed Henry, "for I never have been much good at this game. I was telling the Duke only yesterday that James has always been the best player of my acquaintance, and that it was quite unfair for him to win so often when I never seemed to improve no matter how much I practised."

A smile tugged at the corner of James' mouth as a memory of her aged fourteen sprang to mind, where she was stretched out on the floor with her face creased up in concentration as she tried desperately to free the toy ladder from the pile of jack-straws.

"That's because you always tried to acquire the highest scoring pieces instead of the ones you could remove easily."

She rolled her eyes. "Well, why would I settle for a measly two points when I could win ten?"

"Because you could acquire more points in the long game."

"Pooh," she said, apparently unconcerned at her rudeness as the gentlemen in the room all laughed. "I demand you join in the match, James. I'll bet you five shillings that I'll beat you in the end."

"I'll bet ten shillings on Lord Cottingham to be

the winner and beat you all soundly," said the Marchioness, effectively giving the game her blessing.

"While I have ten on Lady Henrietta," added Lady Lade. "Shall I run the book?"

"Challenge accepted," he said and was rewarded with a room full of cheers.

"I'm in," said the Duke, smiling down at Henry in a way that, for some unknown reason, James found that he did not quite like. "But I only feel it's fair to warn you that I was a master at jackstraws in my youth."

"But that was so long ago," said Henry, her face a picture of innocence, even as the inhabitants of the room burst into peals of laughter.

"Wretch!" laughed Devenish, and he flicked her under the chin. "I'll fleece you of your entire fortune just for that comment, and then make you drive me down to Merton while I crow about my victory the entire way."

James frowned as the table was pulled out more players stepped forward to join in the initial game. He had no idea where the box of jackstraws came from, but within moments Henry was dropping them onto the centre of the table, while furious betting began amongst the spectators.

It was as though the Henry of his childhood - impulsive, fun, and utterly wild - has crash landed before him in the form of a pretty twenty-year-old, and for some reason, he resented the fact that the surrounding gentlemen were on the receiving end of her humour and high spirits. He'd become so used to her as a refined but colourless debutante that he's somehow forgotten who she used to be.

Who she had always been.

"Ten points to start!" she cried out in triumph, waving the key-hole saw above her head to a mixture of cheers and groans. "Are you so sure you can best me now?"

"I'll do my best," said James, as that odd sensation in the pit of his stomach returned.

*

Although she was knocked out of the jackstraws tournament at the end of the first game, Henrietta was grateful for the opportunity to fetch herself a glass of lemonade away from the eyes of the guests. Everyone was so deeply engrossed in the final round that it seemed no one noticed her take a place on the window seat, alone with her thoughts.

Why oh why did he have to look so devastatingly handsome as he played the silly children's game with so much seriousness she almost believed he cared about the outcome? Of course, she knew it was his naturally competitive spirit - he had never let her win as children, after all - but a tiny part of her wanted to believe that he was desperate for her to drive him to Merton.

Henrietta glanced over at Miss Juneberry as she enthusiastically cheered James on, and not for the first time, thought what a splendid couple they would make.

"Is everything well, my dear?" asked Devenish as he settled himself beside her. Henrietta looked up at him with a smile.

"I should have guessed that you would notice my slipping away from the crowd."

"Well, I do hate to be bored," he said a touch apologetically, "so naturally I gravitate to the most interesting person in any room."

Henrietta rolled her eyes. "I've told you a thousand times not to try to buy me with your Spanish coin, Devenish; I'll not take it!"

"You really don't take compliments well, do you?" he said with a shake of his head. "Very well, I want your opinion on whether I was foolish backing Mr Filey to win. He seemed a promising opponent, but is flagging at the final mile."

"James will probably win," she replied, and sounded sulky even to her own ears.

Devenish raised an eyebrow. "Still unable to take your childhood friend's victory with good spirits?"

She tried to smile, glad that he had misunderstood the source of her melancholy. "Do we ever outgrow such rivalries?"

"Quite possibly not, my dear, but I'm sure he would refrain from rubbing your nose in the dirt if you were forced to drive him to Merton alongside you."

It was all she could do to repress a shudder.

She knew on an intellectual level that James had no interest in her as a prospective bride and was thus quite openly looking to make a match elsewhere. However, she found that even the thought of him discussing another female with her, such as Amelia Juneberry, in warm terms made her want to throw herself into the river Wandle.

"He'd probably chide me for taking a corner too quickly or some such thing."

There was a sudden bout of whoops and cheers from the table that drew their attention back to the game.

"Miss Manning wins!" cried Lady Lade. "I'll be damned if I'd not thought to back such a sly filly!"

Henrietta ran over to Beatrix and gave her friend a tight hug, genuinely relieved that she had won.

"Congratulations - and I promise most faithfully that I shall not turn you into a ditch!"

Beatrix laughed and hugged her right back. "I will be the envy of London, I am sure!"

"Normally I'd be green with jealousy," said Lady Cordelia, "but as experience has taught me that my cousin is a regular captain sharp when it comes to jackstraws, I laid twenty shillings on her to win and have quite cleaned up!"

The conversation stayed lively as people began to debate who was going to take a carriage on the trip to Merton, and who intended to ride. Henrietta was naturally no part of this discussion, and before she even realised what had happened, found herself back at the window seats, only this time James was beside her.

"Would that I had won the game," he said ruefully. "It's been an age since we spent any time together, Henry, and there is so much I want to talk to you about."

Henrietta started to panic, more convinced than ever that she was not ready to listen to James sing the praises of some other female. "Oh yes I'm sure I've so much to tell you as well, Devenish and I came up with a simply fabulous scheme to-"

"I don't want to talk about His Grace," replied James with a frown. "You are always running about with that fellow, and I can barely get two minutes of your time."

His terse words brought out some of her spirit, and she glared back at him. "My apologies if I am no longer at your beck and call, Lord Cottingham, but since I had to find ways to amuse myself during the year you were away I discovered that I enjoy partaking of the amusements London has to offer."

"You didn't know Devenish from Adam until this Season," he said.

"No, but I did know Lord Standish, and Mr Filey, and Sir Richard, and Cordy and Trix and even your precious Miss Juneberry, all of whom are ready to make time to spend with me on my terms just as surely as I am willing to spend time on theirs. His Grace may be a new friend but he is a dear one, and I'd thank you to remember that he at least takes the time to ask me about my thoughts and is actually interested enough to respond."

"I…, of course, I'm interested in your wishes!" he replied, appearing taken aback by her words.

"Such as remembering to read a single one of my letters, or to bring me back a little souvenir from Montreal, or recollect when we are to ride together without needing me to send you a note," she said bitterly. For the first time, she wished that they were alone if only to be able to shout at him the way she wanted.

"Henry, are you still so upset at me about those cursed letters?"

"Not in the least," she replied, her traitorous eyes threatening to spill over. "Now, please excuse me, I have something of great import to ask His Grace, and as everyone will be leaving soon, it cannot wait another moment."

She walked blindly across the room, a bright smile plastered on her face as she made her way to Devenish, who had taken a seat beside Grandpapa.

"I must thank you for your intervention, my dear Lady Henrietta, for the Marquis has consented to allow me to ride his Cassidus down to Merton."

"With no guarantee that I will sell," added Grandpapa, "but at my age, one has to think of such things, and as exquisite a whip as you are, my girl, I'll not have you on the back of that hell beast."

"I thought you'd promised him to Sir John?" she asked, but Grandpapa just laughed.

"Cassidus tried to bite him, and he said that there were easier horses to bring to the bridle."

"That's true enough," said Devenish with a small smile, "but I appreciate a challenge."

The two men laughed, and Henrietta joined in. Devenish looked at her sharply.

"I say, are you quite well, my dear?"

"Oh, I'm just still in a fit of sullens for losing the game, and not entirely sure that I am happy with my contribution to the Literary Gathering, either."

"I find myself labouring under a similar cloud," he said quite seriously, which at least made her laugh.

"As if anything you read out would be less than amusing. Ah, I see our guests are starting to leave, Grandpapa. I suppose I must go and do the pretty!"

She managed to hold it together well enough that she doubted anyone in the room was aware of her inner turmoil, even as James left without coming to say goodbye to her after bidding adieu to her grandmother. Although normally this would have crushed her, the fact that he had Amelia Juneberry on his arm made her rather glad.

"Are you sure you are happy for me to drive with you on the Merton trip?" asked Beatrix before she took her leave, and Henrietta squeezed her hand in response.

"My dearest friend, I couldn't think of a single person I'd rather have sitting up beside me for the drive," she replied, and for the first time that afternoon was being perfectly honest.

CHAPTER TEN

James found himself unable to get his thoughts in order, even hours after he had left the Shropshire's home. He dashed off a note to William and Herbert to cancel their plans for the evening, and instead took himself off to his library to think through what had happened with Henry over the last few weeks.

No, that wasn't fair. It was the last few years he needed to think through, including the fact that he's never taken the time to reply to any of her letters, and then left her to her assumption that he'd never opened them at all. Her last, heated words to him had hurt - not least because he recognised the truth in them. Just when had he taken to assuming she'd be available whenever he called? Or stopping valuing her opinion, when everyone knew she was a dashed intelligent girl. Somehow their relationship had changed from one of friends on an equal footing to that of an arrogant young Lord confident of his place in the world, and the young woman of genteel birth that he paid little mind to.

It was not a pleasant reflection.

He was still mulling the situation over with the help of a brandy glass when he heard his mother return home from her card party, and was surprised to discover that it was already midnight.

"James, is that you? I thought you were engaged to spend the evening with Lord Standish and Mr Filey? Don't tell me you humbugged me to get out of attending Lady Warren's gathering? I have told you several times that although her young sister-in-law is a very wealthy heiress, I would never seriously consider promoting a match between the two of you, as the girl is as spoiled as the day is long!"

"I simply had a lot to think about, and it wasn't something I wished to discuss with Herbert and William," he replied.

His mother studied him in silence for a long moment, and then went across to the decanter to pour herself a brandy. "Is it Henrietta?" she asked as the amber liquid sloshed into her glass.

"Why would it be Henry?" he asked, but his mother just rolled her eyes.

"Don't try to gammon me, my darling. The tow

of you have been at outs ever since you arrived back in London - and it's not as though I'm the only person who noticed it! The Marchioness and even Lady Loughcroft have voiced their concerns to me about whatever falling out the two of you have had."

"We haven't fallen out," he said, and then with a moment's reflection, added: "at least, not a falling out to set us at sixes and sevens. Ever since she told me that she was determined to snag a husband this Season, everything has been going wrong between us."

"Is that how it happened?" asked his mother, her tone serene as she contemplated the brandy.

"Yes, she told me that-" he stopped, replaying that first visit so many weeks ago over in his mind. "No, you're right. She told me that she'd turned down a number of offers and that they were all writing ghastly poetry to her - William and Herbert included, would you believe? - and I told her that maybe it was time to consider marriage after all."

His mother raised one delicate eyebrow. "How uncivil of you."

"I don't know about uncivil - she's practically family, after all."

"Good Lord, of course it was uncivil! You insinuated that she was an ape leader."

"Of course she isn't a dashed ape leader! I just

meant that it was high time for her to look about for a husband."

"Which she's been doing - and very well, from what the Marchioness tells me. Devenish has certainly been dancing attendance upon her."

"That rascal!" said James, and took a long drink of his brandy.

"I'll have you know that the Duke is a very kind man, James, and that silly nickname has been twisted out of all original meaning."

"I can't believe that he has serious intentions toward Henry!"

"Why? Because you do not?"

James practically dropped his glass, only just managing to save it before he sent the brandy spilling all down his breeches. His mother sipped at her glass, but her eyes were trained on him.

"I've known her since she was in leading strings," he said.

"Yes, and I've often heard it said that familiarity leads to contempt, or at the very least blinds one to the qualities of another. You have become very used to Henrietta being at your beck and call over the years, James, and I have told you a thousand times to value her more than you have done."

"She... she was just Henry," he said, and even to

his own ears, he sounded like a spoiled wretch.

"I'm well aware of that, and as much as it pains me to see you hurt, my darling, I think it would be a very good thing for Henrietta to marry a gentleman who valued her spirit and intellect instead of encouraging her to be an insipid miss."

"I never encouraged that!"

"No? You praised her when she behaved meekly and teased her whenever she showed a dash of personality. If you are trying to tell me that you have been unaware of the fact that Henrietta has been hopelessly in love with you since she was 8 years old, then quite frankly, you're blind."

He stared at his mother for what felt like twenty solid minutes as she took another sip from her brandy.

"I- no, it would only be a half-truth to say I didn't know."

"It was the condition of your own heart that you were unaware of, I take it?"

James leant back in his chair and closed his eyes. "I still don't. All I know is that I've made a dashed mull of things, and if Henry never speaks to me again, I shall have no one to blame but myself."

"Yes, I would tend to agree with that assessment."

He opened his eyes and met her gaze. "You are not much of a comfort."

"And why should I be? You are a man after all, and a peer of the realm. You have taken Henrietta for granted all of your life, as well you know. Lord, I didn't know where to look when the Marchioness told me that you had never so much as sent the poor girl a note while you were in Montreal, or made the time to purchase her even the smallest of gifts!"

"I was…" he began, but stopped himself before finishing the lie. "No, I wasn't too busy to respond. It's just that by the time I'd finished her letter I would set it aside with every intention of responding, but then there would always be some other distraction, and before I knew it, her next letter had arrived, and I'd start the process all over again."

"It's no wonder that she chooses to spend so much time with Devenish," said his mother with a sigh. "I had cherished hopes for the two of you, but I regret to say that I believe the Duke would treat her a dashed sight better than you have done!"

"Is it too late, do you think?" he blurted out, and came under the intense scrutiny of his parent.

She placed the glass on the table beside her and then stood. James waited in desperate silence as she smoothed out her skirts.

"I have no reason to believe that His Grace has

made an offer of marriage to Henrietta, just as I have no reason to believe that she would accept it. However, I don't think that is quite what you meant, and the answer there is that I am not sure. When you first returned she might have forgiven you, but now?" she shook her head. "You know her better than I do, James. For your sake, I hope she is not against your suit."

She bent over his chair and kissed the top of his head as though he were still a young boy in need of his mother's love.

"If anyone can think of a way to apologise to Henrietta and beg a second chance it is you, my love," she said softly, and then left the library, closing the door softly behind her.

James spent a few minutes more thinking about her words before pulling himself up to his feet.

"Where did I put them?" he murmured to himself, frowning first at the bookshelves and then next at his desk. A faint memory flared, and he soon found himself digging through the right-hand drawer until he uncovered a small packet of letters bound together with a blue ribbon.

He returned to his chair, tugging gently at the ribbon until the letters fell loose into his lap. He picked up the first one, the paper smooth beneath his fingers, and leant back into his seat as he began to read.

"My dearest James…"

*

William Standish finished reciting his poem and then gave a deep, flourishing bow as everyone collapsed into fits of laughter.

"I'm flattered, truly," said the Duchess, barely keeping her mirth in check.

"I've half a mind to call you out just for making her sit through that hogwash," said Devenish, but he was smiling as he said it.

James risked a glance over at Henry, who seemed to be enjoying herself immensely. She had showcased her own talents by reading them a simply awful sonnet listing all the reasons she hated Shakespeare, and received a standing ovation as a result.

It was without a doubt the strangest party he had ever been to, and under other circumstances, he would likely have found it a great deal of fun. The Duchess had indifferent health it was true, but she was a remarkable hostess full of wit and ready to be pleased. The ladies present were naturally gregarious, and he was surprised to see Miss Juneberry in such an animated state. The gentlemen were all known to him, so he had not doubted they would be entertaining. Even Devenish, who he fervently wanted to dislike, was proving himself to have a dry sense of humour that had an easy appeal.

But then he would glance over at Henry who was doing her level best not to look at him, and he felt something in his heart crumble.

Was this how she'd felt over the last few years as he remained indifferent to her many qualities? How about every day that had passed while he was in Canada; had she waited for a letter until the very end, or had she given up on him long before his return?

"My turn!" announced Lady Cordelia as she got to her feet and began reciting from her play in a grave manner so at odds with the material that she had everyone in absolute whoops.

James laughed along with everyone else, but his mind refused to come to heel. He thought about all of those beautiful, playful letters that Henry had sent him while in Canada, not one berating his lack of response.

He'd fallen slowly into their magic as he'd read her witty descriptions of some dowager's hat before moving on to an earnest discussion about a quarrel she'd had with a chimney sweep over his treatment of a climbing boy, and some information on sweeping changes to the estate management that her Grandpapa had implemented.

It had hit him like a punch in the gut when he realised what he stood at risk of losing. Henry was, and always would be, an engaging hoyden that it was his privilege to know – and now he stood on the cusp of losing her.

A thunderous round of applause recalled him to the present, and he clapped loudly for Lady Cordelia, even though he had little idea as to what everyone had found so thoroughly amusing.

"That was splendid," said Henry, wiping a tear from her eye.

Lady Cordelia sighed heavily as she dropped into her chair, her face a picture of morose dejection. "You may laugh all you please, for it makes it more and more apparent that my career as a literary dramatist has died before it was ever born."

"There, there," said Miss Manning as she patted her cousin on the knee. "You can aspire to be a great comedienne instead."

The Duchess smiled at them indulgently, and then turned her attention to James. "And what about you, Lord Cottingham? What have you brought to the Literary Gathering of Dubious Merit?"

James stood, cleared his throat, and then did his best to smile at everyone in the room. His hands were shaking, but thankfully, the paper that he clutched did not rustle too loudly.

"As some of you may be aware, it is a secret ambition of mine to become a man of letters famous enough to rival Sir Horace Walpole," he began. Almost everyone laughed, but he couldn't bring himself to look at Henry to gauge her reaction.

"Yes, we all enjoyed your considerable volume of correspondence while you were away," said William, which caused another round of laughter.

James felt his cheeks heating but tried to retain an appearance of nonchalance.

"Precisely, William. With that in mind, I thought I would read you perhaps the most important letter I have ever written."

"It sounds delightful already," said the Duchess with an encouraging smile. "Please do read it to us."

James cleared his throat again and shifted his weight from foot to foot a few times. When the ground did not answer his prayers by opening up and swallowing him whole, he gave the sheets of paper a decided shake and began.

My darling girl,

I imagine that you are quite appalled at my shocking lack of replies during the last twelvemonth, and have imagined all kinds of terrible fates for me. I beg your leave to reassure you that I have not been eaten by bears or any other wildlife, that I have not had the good fortune to meet with any of the natives of this wonderful land, and more by luck than good sense have avoided being frozen to death by the cold winter winds of Montreal.

The Foolish Friend

The people here are friendly and lively in a way that only those used to prolonged periods of cold can be, and I have discovered a fondness for fur muffs that I admit I never thought I would have gained. My brother jokes that we look like bear cubs as we totter through the snowy streets clad head to toe in beaver pelts, while those born and raised here dress more fitted for a late afternoon stroll that the frigid conditions of Upper Canada. I often find myself turning to address a remark to you about our ridiculousness or expect to see you coming out of a shop only to laugh at me and call me a foolish boy. It is in these moments - and please believe me when I say they happen daily - that I realise that we are oceans apart, and I remember that I am no longer quite whole.

Did you know that I look forward to receiving and reading your letters? Do not ask me what they all contain, for I have treated them very ill and consume them like a thirsty man happening upon a glass of water. They satiate a need I cannot bring myself to name, but when they are done, I set them aside, never to be looked at again. Not because I dislike them, but for the opposite reason. I am afraid that I enjoy them too much, and if I must think of how long we have been apart, and are yet to be apart, then I know I will unman myself and weep tears that will freeze to my lashes, and betray my soul to my casual acquaintances in Montreal.

So, after a year with not so much as a line from me to tell you that I am alive, I must cut this letter short for fear of losing myself in it. I miss you, my darling girl, and all the absurd pranks and tricks that you would inevitably draw me into where I there to partake in them.

Dance with every wretch foolish enough to so-licit the hand of a goddess for a set, laugh with Your Grace-filled friends and let the Ton fall head over heels in love with you. Just remember - you still aren't allowed to drive my bays.

Ever Yours,

James

There was a long silence as he lowered the paper, and he glanced first to the Duchess, whose eyes glistened.

"My Lord Cottingham, I'm afraid to tell you there was much, much merit to your letter," she said softly.

Her words gave him encouragement, and he turned to face Henry with a hopeful smile on his face.

Like the Duchess, her eyes glistened.

But it was not because he had moved her with his words.

"How. Dare. You," she breathed at him, her

voice caught between a growl and a sob. Her cheeks were flushed as she rose to her feet, her balled fists shaking at her sides.

"Henry," he began, but there were no more words to say as she held up one hand before her.

"You go too far," she said, then turned and left the room.

There was a long moment where everyone froze in place, as though trying to digest what had just happened.

Miss Manning recovered first, jumping to her feet and following Henry, calling over her shoulder: "I'll go see if I can be of use to her."

"I will come as well," said Lady Cordelia, pausing only to throw a thoughtful glance at James before she disappeared from the room.

"Well. Perhaps you shouldn't write letters, after all, dear chap," said William with a weak smile. A few people laughed dutifully, but their tone was subdued.

James turned to the Duchess and bowed deeply. "Your Grace, I am so sorry to have inconvenienced you in such a manner and caused upset to one of your guests. I am aware of how much you were looking forward to this gathering, and I promise most faithfully not to disrupt this or any future party of yours again. Your servant, ma'am."

He did not give her a chance to reply before turning on his heel and walking quickly from the room - quite deliberately choosing a different door from the one Henry and her friends had used. He wasn't quite sure how he managed to request his hat and gloves from the butler, but they were being pressed into his hands when an unexpected voice stopped him from leaving the house.

"Cottingham, please allow me five minutes of your time, if you will. There's something I would like to discuss with you in my study."

James looked up and met the piercing gaze of the Duke, and knew that the older man would not take no for an answer. He felt like a hunting dog at his master's heels as he followed the Duke into his office, and did his best not to wince as Devenish firmly clicked the door shut.

"No doubt you wish to tell me to go to the devil for disrupting a much-anticipated event for your mother," James began, "and you have every right to do it. I've been wishing myself there for the past five minutes and do not plan to stop in the near future."

"Do you love her?"

The simple question stopped James in his tracks. He stared at the Duke as His Grace inspected some papers on his desk.

"I'm not sure I follow."

"It was a simple enough question," said Devenish, turning his attention back to James with a piercing gaze that made him want to look away. "Do you love her?"

"I... that is... well, that is I'm not sure it's any of your business, Your Grace."

"On the contrary, my boy, it very much is my business. Amongst other things, I have promised Lady Loughcroft that her cousin will not come to any harm under my care. Your actions in there will undoubtedly result in a fair measure of gossip, which I can only deal with when I understand your intent in this matter. So I ask you again, Lord Cottingham: do you love her?"

James closed his eyes, but the world continued to pitch and buck all around him.

"Yes," he said quietly. "I have loved her since she was eight years old, and stood before me like a brave tiger cub as I untangled a caterpillar from her hair that my own brother had put there. She was terrified, but so determined to be one of the boys no matter how much they played tricks upon her, and I fell in love with her even though I never knew it to be the case."

The Duke regarded him in silence for a long while. Eventually, he walked over to the low-burning fireplace, where he pulled some folded sheets of paper from his chest pocket and consigned them to the flames.

"Your Grace?" said James by way of enquiry, but the Duke flashed him a sardonic smile.

"It was to be my contribution to the Gathering, but it would hardly be appropriate now even if the party were not likely to break up in light of today's drama."

"I see," said James, not sure in the least why the Duke was acting in such a strange manner.

"Well, I won't keep you any longer, Cottingham, but I do hope to see you at the occasional gathering in the future."

"Thank you for the invitation," he replied, recognising a dismissal when he heard one. He was at the door of the study when the Duke spoke again.

"Cottingham? I trust you will still be a part of the Merton expedition tomorrow, won't you?"

"I hardly think that Henry will be disappointed if I renege," James said, his heart heavy as he thought about it.

"On the contrary, I think you will make a bad situation impossible if you do. Lady Henrietta appears to be labouring under the assumption that you are indifferent to her, and I strongly believe that she took your letter to be a mocking one rather than in the spirit you intended it. Merton will offer you a chance to fix your mistake."

James stared at the Duke as the sound logic in the older man's words hit him forcefully.

Then he remembered who he was talking to, and frowned.

"Why would you help me?"

"I told you, I promised Lady Loughcroft that her cousin would come to no harm through her association with me. I'm tolerably certain that includes losing the love of her life. Now I must return to my guests - I trust you can see yourself out?"

"Of course Your Grace," said James, looking at the Duke with new eyes as he wondered how such a splendid man could have earned the nickname Devilish.

CHAPTER ELEVEN

To a casual observer, it would have appeared as though the entire Ton had decided to take a trip to Merton that morning, with the first group of carriages and riders assembling at Hanover Square.

Grandpapa's barouche was positioned outside of the family mansion, while Henrietta's curricle was immediately behind. Their horses had been groomed to perfection, and short of Prinny turning up with six-in-hand to join their party, Henrietta was convinced they could not look more bang-up if they tried.

Several people had chosen to ride to Merton rather than drive, including Lord Standish and Mr Filey. Henrietta was more concerned, however, when Devenish rode into Hanover Square on no other beast but Cassidus, her grandfather's prized but spirited stallion.

He was, without a doubt, the most beautiful horse the Shropshire stables had ever produced, but her Grandpapa was too old to take control of the beast, and he'd already broken the shoulder of one of their grooms with a well placed, powerful kick.

"Are you sure it's the best idea to bring Cassidus along for the ride?" she asked her Grandpapa as the horse bucked beneath Devenish, trying to throw him off.

"The Duke can handle a bit of playfulness," replied her Grandpapa before patting her on the hand. "Besides, if he's going to pay through the nose for the cantankerous beast, I'd have a clearer conscience if he knew exactly what he was purchasing in advance.

"I think it ill-advised," Henrietta said with a small shake of her head, "but if Devenish thinks he can handle Cassidus, who am I to stop him breaking his neck?"

"Your sensibility is overwhelming," laughed Grandpapa, and he handed her up into her carriage before going to hand the Marchioness up into his barouche.

With only a handful of false starts, the small convoy - led by Lord Shropshire and his team of four high-steppers - made their way to Green Park only half an hour later than planned, and there met up with the rest of the party.

Henrietta could barely keep her smile contained as she saw the sheer number of people who had accepted her grandparents' invitation to attend the "small" picnic at Merton. It appeared that when Lord and Lady Shropshire requested the presence of the Ton at an entertainment, regardless as to whether it was on shockingly short notice or not, the Ton responded en masse.

Her cousin Emma and Loughcroft were in a smart curricle, while the Lades followed in a spanking high-perch phaeton that Henrietta coveted on sight. Lady Cordelia and her parents were in their family barouche, as were the Seftons, the Jerseys, and a whole host of other families. Lord Standish and Mr Filey were both riding showy mounts, as were many other gentlemen (and a few ladies) who had joined the cavalcade, and Devenish kept a little way apart from everyone, but seemed immensely pleased with Cassidus.

"I have never been more grateful for my innate skill at jackstraws," declared Beatrix from the seat beside Henrietta. "I feel like royalty, riding with you!"

"You look it as well!" replied Henrietta with a genuine smile. Her friend's jonquil pelisse was not the height of fashion and had likely seen a few years of wear, but the colour suited her and, paired with a pretty bonnet, she really did look quite lovely.

"It was a stroke of luck that your Grandpapa chose red for your curricle, not to mention that ravishing riding habit," Beatrix said with a happy smile. "I re-trimmed my bonnet with red and yellow ribbons just so that I would complement you."

"And you do so perfectly," said Henrietta, determined to be cheerful and happy despite everything. "I should be thanking you for making my curricle look even more dashing!"

Lord Shropshire set a clipping pace on the drive down to Merton, and it felt good to match his prowess in her own curricle rather than having to beg for the chance to handle the ribbons. Beatrix was an entertaining companion and was kind enough not to ask about the shocking events the day before.

Before Henrietta felt that she had really had a chance to put her new carriage through its paces, they had arrived at Kelwick Manor. The property rightly belonged to the Marchioness, and although it was hardly necessary considering the dazzling array of homes owned by the Shropshires, it was a particularly charming house at the centre of fifty acres that held fond memories for every last one of Henrietta's relatives.

An army of servants - many sent down from the London mansion the night before - stood ready to receive the guests, and she noted with satisfaction that her Grandpapa had thought ahead and brought one of the grooms familiar with Cassidus along to help the Duke. Glasses of chilled champagne were handed out to each member of the party, and everyone was gently guided over to the lawn where picnic blankets and cushions awaited them. A string quartet was playing beneath some oak trees, and footmen stood ready to serve a dazzling array of delectable treats for everyone.

"I have died and gone to heaven," declared Lady Cordelia as she dropped onto the picnic blanket between Beatrix and Henrietta. "As much as I love my parents, I think I want to be adopted by Lord and Lady Shropshire."

"Have you tried the salmon?" Beatrix demanded. "Believe me, you haven't gone to heaven if you are yet to have a mouthful."

Henrietta just smiled, used to her grandparent's lavish style of entertainment, but still appreciative.

Lord Standish came bounding over with all the enthusiasm of a poorly trained puppy.

"Lord Shropshire has set up an archery tournament down beside the river," he announced, practically bouncing on the spot. "Do say you'll come and join in, Lady Cordelia? I've laid a pony on you to beat Herbert."

"Does he still believe he's a better shot than

me?" said Cordy as she climbed to her feet. She was smiling, but there was a martial gleam in her eyes.

"He says you wouldn't be able to shoot an apple, even if he attached it to your arrow first," said Lord Standish, with a blatant disregard for the truth that went straight over Cordy's head.

"We shall see about that!" she declared, and began marching off toward the river, Lord Standish at her side.

Beatrix climbed to her feet with a sigh.

"I'd better go and keep an eye on her before she does something regrettable," she said, and ran off after her cousin.

Henrietta laughed and shook her head as she watched them go.

"Do you think your grandfather will sell me any more of his cattle?" asked Devenish as he dropped onto the blanket beside her. "Cassidus may be a brute, but by God, he's the best horse I've ridden in an age."

"Not a chance, I'm afraid. He's willed most of his stock to my cousin Gloucester upon his death, although he has told me that I'll get my pick of his horses first."

"Then I'll simply have to marry you then," he said, and something in the tone of his voice made her turn to look at him.

"Careful, Your Grace, I might accept your offer and then where will you be?"

"I can imagine a worse fate," he said with a smile that didn't quite form on his lips, "but I think that is not where your heart lies, now is it?"

"I, I don't know what you mean," Henrietta said, looking everywhere but directly at the Duke.

"Yes, you do," he replied.

They sat in uncomfortable silence for the longest time.

"I-" began Henrietta, but Devenish held up one hand to stay her speech.

"There can be nothing gained from giving voice to those thoughts, my dear. I will be retiring to Bath early next week with my mother so that she can drink the waters. I have enjoyed living in London, but it is starting to bore me and that, as you know, will never do."

"I'm sorry," said Henrietta, stomping down on the urge to cry.

The Duke leant over and lifted her chin with one finger, forcing her to look directly into his eyes. For one strange moment, she was sure that he was going to kiss her, but instead, he flashed her a mocking smile.

"Now, what did I tell you about apologising?"

She smiled at that and lifted her chin a little higher.

"You are very fortunate to have known me, Your Grace," she said, and was rewarded with a soft laugh.

"Minx," he said, and then got to his feet and walked over to her grandfather, no doubt to negotiate a price for Cassidus. Henrietta watched him go, her emotions somewhere between relief and sadness.

*

"Am I to wish you happy, then?" James said as he approached Henry. Her back was to him, but he could still see the way she tensed up at the sound of his voice.

"Would you if it were appropriate?" she snapped.

"You know I would," James replied. "For all my flaws, Henry, I have only ever wanted to see you happy."

A bitter laugh escaped her as she clambered to her feet and turned to face him. "No, all you've ever wanted is for me to follow you around like a puppy, ready and willing to receive whatever scraps of affection you throw at me. This isn't a friendship, and it hasn't been for a long time. Good grief, James, do you ever think about me for my own sake? You are so sure of what would make me happy, but never once listened when I tried to tell you about the one thing I thought I needed to achieve it!"

"I think about you all the time," he said, staring into her eyes. "I never realised just how close you were to my thoughts until you no longer needed me around. Does that make me fool?"

"Far worse than that," she said, her eyes blazing. "I cannot blame you for my own behaviours, acting like a simpering miss just because I thought that was what you wanted. But for you to mock me like you did yesterday with that atrocious letter, and in front of my friends and quite possibly your future wife, makes you a rogue, a scoundrel, and a… a damned fool thrice over!"

"Good God Henry, I never mocked you! I meant every word I said!"

"Don't pity me," she half-shouted, and he glanced to his side on reflex to see if anyone had heard. He struggled to rein in his own temper and remain calm.

"I don't pity you, I swear it, and I have no idea why you think I would insult you in front of my future wife since right now it appears she won't have me even if I begged. I'm sorry, truly I am, but perhaps we should take some time to talk in private?"

"No," she replied, lifting her chin a little higher. "No, I'm sick and tired of waiting for you to find time to talk to me, and it's a boat that you have missed, James Douglas. I don't care if you are a Baron or a Duke or a butcher's boy. You are very fortunate to have known me, my Lord, and if you cannot see that, then there is no hope for you. Now please excuse me, I have promised Lady Lade that we will put my curricle through its paces – and I at least keep my promises."

He had no option but to stare at her as she marched away from him and over toward Lady Lade. He looked around, only to meet the sympathetic gaze of Lord Loughcroft, and the amused sneer of Devenish. He ran his hand through his hair, unsure as to what to do or where to go.

"Foolish boy," said Lady Loughcroft as she stepped up beside him. "What on earth made you think you should try to talk with her now?"

He couldn't resist looking over at Devenish, who was now animatedly talking with the Marquis. "I thought, perhaps, it was too late."

Henry and Lady Lade were walking toward the cherry-red curricle, the latter with barely-contained enthusiasm for both the carriage and the horses.

"Men really are such fools," sighed Emma. "So not it appears I must meddle after all. What you need to do is sweep her off her feet, do something dashing. Aren't you coming to the masquerade?"

"What? Yes, yes, of course. The Fitzburgh's are related to my mother."

The two women climbed up into the curricle, the reins and whip firmly in Henry's hands as the end of her riding habit dangled out of the seat beside her.

"Even better! We can arrange for something utterly romantic, such as-"

"I'm sorry, will you forgive me, Lady Loughcroft, but there's something I must attend to," said James, as he started walking quickly toward the front of the house where Henry was preparing to set off. She might not want to talk with him, but her cape stood a very real risk of tangling in the wheel – and for some god-unknown reason the footman was oblivious.

"Henry! Lady Lade!" he shouted, picking up his pace. Henry glared in his direction and then set the horses to, moving at a clipping pace right out of the gate. Fear gripped at James' throat as he realised her cloak was flapping hard against the front carriage wheel.

"Henry!" he yelled, caring not that everyone must be looking at him as he ran hell-for-leather across the lawn and grabbed the reins of the nearest horse. He threw himself up into the saddle and lashed out at the stable hand who tried to stop him.

"Damn you man, can't you see I'm trying to prevent an accident?" he shouted as he dug his heels into the horse's flank.

But it appeared he had made a poor choice of steed, for the animal reared suddenly, and then began to buck and jump in a violent attempt to dislodge him.

James swore roundly, gripping on tightly to the saddle's pommel as he was aware of people shouting and screaming all around him. The horse brayed loudly and threw itself high in the air once more, and James had only a moment to see the ground hurtling toward him at a frightening, unstoppable pace.

CHAPTER TWELVE

"Careful of your dress, my dear," said Lady Lade as they turned the first corner of the driveway.

"Oh thank you, I'd have been monstrously upset if it ripped," replied Henrietta as she tugged the hem of her skirts back up into the carriage.

"Occupation hazard," said Lady Lade, "but now that the danger is passed - let's see just how fast your horses are!"

Their ride was glorious, and Henrietta lost herself in the pounding of the horse's hooves, the laughter of her companion and the joy of handling the ribbons.

"By God, you're a damned fine driver!" shouted Lady Lade, and Henrietta felt her chest swell with pride. At that moment, she cared about nothing and no one as all her cares were left behind her as they disappeared into the trees. Lady Lade gave a whoop of joy, and Henrietta laughed out loud, not caring if it was vulgar or poor Ton to just enjoy the moment as they thundered along the driveway, branches and leaves whipping just a hair's breadth above their bonnets as the breeze pinched at their cheeks and noses.

She took the final corner with less than an inch to spare, Lady Lade's encouragement making her push her skill to the limit. Although she knew that her reputation as a driver would be cemented by that Lady's praise to the Ton, she was conscious of a tiny thought that made her wish everyone could witness her skills in the same manner.

They began the circle back toward the house, her beautiful chestnut horses responding to her demanding pace as though it were their only passion and purpose in life.

"It will be a pleasure driving back to London with you," announced Lady Lade, "and I predict that you will never want for people to tool about Hyde Park with you, my dear Lady Henrietta. You simply must come to our estate this summer so I can try my skill against yours."

"A race?" Henrietta asked, startled and delighted by the idea.

Perhaps it was not the most Ladylike of things

to do, but her Grandmama had certainly taken part in competitions on private land so it could not be considered beyond the pale, surely?

"I would need Grandpapa's permission, of course, but it sounds monstrously good fun!"

"Capital! We can- Good God, what do you suppose has got into your grandfather's Cassidus?"

They had turned back toward the house, where they could see a crowd of people gathered on the edge of the lawn. On the driveway, just before the carriages, Cassidus was jumping and bucking, doing his level best to avoid the attention of a group of men that appeared to be trying to capture his reins. Two other gentlemen carried a third up the stairs and into the house before she could make out who the injured party was.

A feeling of dread built up in Henrietta's chest as they raced up the driveway back toward the house.

"No, oh no," she murmured, and then set the horses thundering at a pace she didn't even know was possible.

"What happened? Who is hurt? Tell me!" she demanded as she pulled up just in front of the main house. Cassidus was back under control and in the hands of Sir John and Devenish, but a large number of people milling about on the driveway made it impossible to tell who was missing. With a curse, she thrust the reins into the hands of an astonished Lady Lade, and then jumped down to the ground.

Beatrix was at her side in a moment.

"I'm so sorry, but it's Lord Cottingham. He tried to ride Cassidus although none of us know why, but that foul-tempered beast threw him at the first opportunity. He is conscious and seems well enough, but the Marquis has sent for a doctor just in case. I'm not sure what will happen to the horse, but Devenish and Sir John seem to have him in hand."

"Nothing will happen to Cassidus!" declared Henrietta, the sensation of dread fading to be replaced by white-hot rage. "What a fool to try and ride such a horse – and I'll have you know, Beatrix Manning, that he isn't foul-tempered in the slightest when in the hand of a nonpareil – as Sir John is demonstrating quite beautifully! Did they take James inside? Oh, just wait until I get my hands on that... on that idiot!"

She pushed aside her dumbfounded friend and marched into the house, following the noise of a small commotion until she found herself in the front parlour. James had been laid out on the sofa where a large number of people seemed to be clucking about him and not actually doing anything of purpose. Her grandparents stood off to one side in conversation with the Loughcrofts and Lady Cottingham, while several staff members hovered in the centre of the room, apparently unsure of their role in the drama but wanted to be a part of it nonetheless.

"Ladies I appreciate your efforts, but really, I do not need my forehead to be bathed in lavender water," James said through gritted teeth as Cordy and Miss Juneberry both fussed over him.

A tiny part of Henrietta realised that she would normally have found this picture hilarious, but the fires that had been stoked inside of her were burning white-hot and demanded release.

"Of all the idiotic, cow handed, bumble-headed and downright ridiculous pranks I have ever heard you try to pull, James Douglas, this is the one that takes the biscuit. How could you have been so stupid as to think that you could handle a horse like Cassidus?" she practically yelled at him.

Everyone turned to look at her, no one daring to utter a word. James seemed as surprised as everyone else as she marched further into the room, stripping off her gloves as she did so.

"And how dare you speak to Cordy and Miss Juneberry in such a manner, when they are only trying to ease your suffering? Suffering, I might add, that you absolutely deserve for being such a reckless idiot. I don't care a jot if you hate lavender, you should suffer their ministrations and be grateful."

"Good to know you remember that I hate lavender," he replied softly, something dangerously close to a smirk on his lips. Henrietta glared at him for a moment, and then turned her attention to her grandparents.

"Has he been given laudanum? Or spirits?"

"No, we were waiting for the doctor," replied Grandmama.

"Good," replied Henrietta with considerable venom as she dropped to her knees beside the sofa. "Oh move out of the way, Cordy, if you're going to bathe the brow of a gentleman at least put your backbone into it."

"I- yes, yes, of course," said Cordy, her voice trembling as she moved out of the way. No doubt her nerves were overcome or some such thing, but Henrietta only had space for James in her thoughts right now.

"Do you know," said Lord Loughcroft in an overly-cheerful voice, "I think all these people gawking at Lord Cottingham are making him fretful. What say you, Lord Shropshire? Shall we all retire to the library until the doctor arrives?"

"An excellent suggestion," said Lady Cottingham, with uncharacteristic disregard for her eldest son's wellbeing. "I'm sure my darling Henrietta is perfectly capable of looking after him until then."

"There's no one better," replied the Marquis as everyone – the servants included – suddenly made their way toward the parlour door. "If she doesn't kill him for his stupidity, that is."

Within moments they were alone. Henrietta found her flare of anger had died down into a kind of quiet rage that she was unable to clearly articulate. She jammed the cloth into the bowl of lavender water, hardly caring that the scented liquid sloshed all over the carpets, and then rigorously applied it to James' brow.

"Would you mind not bashing my skull in while you try to gently ease my suffering?" asked James with considerable false humility. "Only Cassidus already tried to break my head open, and he was not as violent about it as you."

"Oh, you absolute wretch!" Henrietta half screamed, and she punched him on the shoulder with the damp cloth.

"That hurt!" he cried out, but his laughter ruined the effect. In fact, for someone who had been thrown from the back of a large and powerful horse, he seemed remarkably well spirited.

"I wish Cassidus had stomped on you," she seethed, her anger coming back. "What on earth did you think you were doing?"

"I was trying to prevent an accident," he said, and the answer caused her to pause.

"You were trying to prevent an accident by riding a horse that you knew full well will try to throw any but the most accomplished of riders," she asked with a frown.

At least he had the good grace to look rueful. "Will you believe me if I said I had no idea it was Cassidus I leapt upon? As you drove off with Lady Lade I realised that your skirts were falling loose beside the carriage wheel, and at the pace you were going I was afraid they'd get tangled, and you'd be dragged out of the curricle. You wouldn't respond when I tried to shout to you, so the only thing I could think of was getting to you as quickly as I could before it happened."

"That's… that's still idiotic," she said, but her anger was already starting to sputter out.

"I know, but at that moment all I could think about was what I would do if some harm were to befall you, about how I could never hope to live without you, because even though I was an idiot-"

"-are an idiot."

"-very well, because even though I am an idiot, and bumble-headed and a wretch-"

"-you forgot cow-handed," she added helpfully.

James burst out into laughter, but then winced in pain.

"Oh dear, are you badly hurt?" she asked, chewing on her lip.

James smiled. "Just bruised I think – and then it's mostly my pride and ego. Mother insisted on a doctor being sent for, but I'm certain nothing's broken."

"That's… good," she said, thinking about all the horrible scenarios she had imagined on the drive back.

James ran a hand through his messy hair. "God, will you ever forgive me, Henry?"

Henrietta stared at her hands. "For trying to ride Cassidus? Of course, for no harm came to him in the end, and Devenish will still likely buy him."

"Minx – you know what I mean. Will you forgive me for being a mutton-headed fool and not realising that I've been in love with you for an absolute age?"

A tiny sob escaped her. "No, you aren't, you just think you are because you've got so used to me being around, to me being yours, that you never even saw me."

"I always saw you," he said, reaching out and pulling her toward him with an insistence that surprised her. "Damn it, Henry, I've always seen you, and I've always admired you. And for the record, I never much like it when you started doing your hair in those demure buns or wearing those missish gowns, but you told me it was all the crack, so I felt compelled to praise them!"

"You never!" she gasped, and he gave a firm nod of his head.

"Indeed I did, even though I was worried you were turning insipid like every other female in London. It worried me, Henry, because it seemed like all the things I liked best about you were the very things you wanted to leave behind in childhood.

"I've been as moody as a bear this Season, not because you were getting the attention you've always deserved, but because I was no longer your partner in crime. Any fool could see Devenish was in love with you, and I've been heartily terrified that you're in love with him, too."

Henrietta felt her cheeks flame. "I'm not in love with His Grace."

"Thank God for that, although if that doesn't prove you're a fool, I don't know what does. He's perfect for you – and well I know it! The thing is, I meant everything that I said yesterday, even if I botched the delivery.

"Henry, I've been an utter fool ever since you

first put up your hair for not realising that there is no woman on this earth that I'd rather marry. If you have me, then I promise to read every note and letter you send me with all the adoration it deserves – even if it's just a reminder to pick up some ribbons for you while I'm in town.

"I'll get involved in any pranks you like so long as they won't irrevocably ruin your reputation, and I'll encourage you to purchase a wardrobe of rainbows if only to keep you out of that insipid white."

"James," she said, half laughing, half sobbing.

"I'll even make sure I untangle every bug that finds its way into your curls and check your bonnet for spiders without you even needing to ask. There's a spider on your bonnet, by the by."

She squealed as she pulled the bonnet from her head and threw it a few feet away from her – only to realise, upon inspection, that she'd been had.

"There's not so much as a flea on my bonnet!" she said indignantly.

"Of course there isn't," said James with a cheerful grin. "There just wasn't any way that I could kiss you with that dashed thing on your head. Come here, you foolish girl."

He pulled her into his arms and kissed her thoroughly, making it very hard to object to his duplicitous behaviour as she melted against him.

"Marry me," he murmured against her mouth. "I don't deserve you, but I swear I'll spend the rest of my life proving to be the best husband you could have wished for. I love you, Henry, and I have done so ever since you were a mud-splattered urchin. Marry me."

"I love you too, and yes I will, I will marry you," she replied, and was rewarded with another heady kiss.

"I do trust that you have honourable intentions, don't you Cottingham?"

Henrietta squeaked with dismay as she half-sprang out of James' arms and turned to face her Grandpapa. She found herself gaping like a freshly caught trout, but James simply sat up and nodded toward the Marquis.

"Indeed I do, Sir; shall I pay you a visit in the morning?"

Grandpapa looked them both up and down with a single eyebrow raised, and then shook his head.

"I've never met such a foolish pair. Very well, Cottingham, you may visit me in the morning to discuss your proposal to my wayward granddaughter. I warn you both in advance, however, that after Gloucester's runaway marriage and the way Emma and Loughcroft tied the knot – well, the less said about that wedding, the better! – but you should both know that the Marchioness is set on marrying off her last grandchild in style. It is the least you can both do after subjecting us all to your starts over the last few years."

"Yes my Lord," said James and Henrietta in unison, then both burst into laughter as the Marquis gave a weary sigh and left them to discuss their future.

NOTES FROM THE AUTHOR

Thank you for reading The Foolish Friend– I hope that you enjoyed it! This is my second book in the Regency Romps Series, and if you have followed on here from The Dashing Widow, I am amazed, thankful and supremely grateful for your continued support.

Whereas my last book was written as a gift to my mum, this story was dedicated to my bestestest friend in the whole entire world, Katie. She has been a constant voice of encouragement about my writing, and although there is an entire ocean and half a continent separating us, she's never more than a phone call away. Katie-doll, you are awesome, and I loves ya.

Although this story is about Henrietta and James, there were several background characters who I really enjoyed writing, and I promise to revisit in later books. This was also the first story that I tried to introduce some actual historical people to. Sir John and Lady Lade were real characters of the Regency period. Both horse-mad, Sir John blew his entire fortune and ended up being made head of the Royal stables just so the Prince Regent could give him an allowance, while Lady Lade had been a courtesan who may have had an ongoing affair with the famous highwayman, Sixteen String Jack, in her youth. She was notorious for having something of a potty mouth – so much so that the Prince Regent was known to call out men who used too many profanities by saying "he swears like Leticia Lade!". As someone who cusses rather more than they should, I have to admit to having a soft spot for the unconventional Letty.

Bluntly, they are two of my favourite people from this time period.

I hope that their inclusion in the book worked for you, and at some point I will do a blog or something about some of the more interesting people who were part of the fabric of London during this time period. As my research collection grows I keep discovering more and more cool things that seem to have been left out of the general history, and that I wish was more generally known.

I have to admit, though, that when it comes to the Regency period I am only an enthusiastic amateur – and therefore I occasionally make mistakes.

To this end, I would like to thank the reviewer, Jenny, who pointed out that in an earlier version of this book I repeatedly had people referring to the Duke of Devenish as "my Lord", which was incorrect. A Duke was and is always referred to as Your Grace, and only as "Lord" in formal writing.

Please, if you find something that I have messed up in the books, such as using the wrong title, or naming a street that wasn't built until the 1900s, please feel free to reach out to me at Elizabeth@ElizabethBramwell.com so that I can correct any errors.

The beauty of indie publishing is that I have the freedom to update at any time, and of course I absolutely adore learning more about this period. I thank every reader who has reached out to me from the bottom of my heart, and it's nice to have made a few friends along the way.

In the meantime, please read on to see the first chapter of my next, His Darling Belle, out now!

Much love,

Beth xxx

His Darling Belle

"Well now, Isabella Snowley, you've really managed to make a mull of things this time, haven't you?" Bella muttered to herself. She stared at the long row of townhouses stretching out in the darkness before her, each one seemingly identical to its neighbours. The thick opera cloak was pulled tight about her shoulders, but the chill wind still found a way to cut right through to her skin.

The plan had seemed so simple a few hours earlier, but now it had become painfully obvious that her rage had masked one tiny but rather important flaw: although she knew that the Earl of Colbourne lived on this street, she had no idea which house was his.

She had never met the man in person as it was rare that he attended society balls, and rumour had it he had never so much as set foot in Almacks – not that it mattered, since she never been granted vouchers for Almacks, anyway.

She knew very little about him, save what she had heard in passing conversations, and would have never given him another thought had circumstances not forced her hand. Her intention of speaking with him in person to ask – no, to demand that he put an end to this petty disagreement with her brother had seemed a noble and worthy endeavour as she crept unseen from her home.

Now, alone in the darkness with a growing sense of her own vulnerability, she was beginning to feel a little foolish, and possibly a little scared.

She stared at the houses for a long time, even taking a few steps along the pavement in the vain hope that somehow, something would indicate to her which house belonged to the Earl of Colbourne. Luck did not favour her, and she struggled to think of a solution. She could hardly go knocking on people's doors at this hour of the night, demanding to know which house belonged to the Earl and insisting that he speak to her at once; such behaviour was the stuff of scandal, and the Lord above knew that her family could not afford any more of that.

Bella sighed. On reflection, she could hardly go knocking on doors demanding an audience with Lord Colbourne at any time of day or night without causing the exact type of scandal she was trying so desperately to avoid. If only the Earl had been the sort to hold balls and functions at his home; she would have had a better idea of his address, and not had to rely on a chance comment from her aunt for direction.

"Come on Bella," she murmured, "there has to be something you can do to get out of this mess. Think, girl, think!"

She bit hard on her lip, enough to taste a small trickle of blood as she walked further down the road. This was too important a mission to abandon, but try as she might she could not think of a way to identify the Earl's home. It was enough to make her want to scream out her frustration; she was so close to her goal but had no way of making the final play of the cards. God alone knew what would happen if she did not at least make an attempt, but there seemed to be no answer.

The sound of voices floated through the darkness. She turned to see two men enter the street, neither appearing to be too steady on his feet and both loudly singing a ditty that made her blush. And they were walking straight towards her.

Panic seized Bella; she pulled down her hood to disguise her face and turned to walk in the opposite direction, but in her haste caught her feet in the hem of her skirts and she tripped. With nothing to steady herself against she fell to the pavement in an inelegant sprawl and ended up tangled in her own cloak.

"Oh, bother," she snapped, struggling to free herself from the folds of velvet threatening to consume her.

"I say, are you alright my dear?" came a voice from somewhere above her.

Bella glanced up. Her hood made it difficult

to see who was speaking, but it was easy enough to guess that the very men she had been trying to avoid had now rushed to help her.

Perfect, she thought bitterly. Just perfect. Now instead of avoiding a family scandal, you've just caused one.

"Hit your head?" said one of the men as he knelt down at her side. Her cloak hood still lay across her face, meaning that she had to tilt her head right back to get a glimpse at him. His voice seemed vaguely familiar, but she couldn't get a good enough look to see if it was someone she knew.

Oh God, please don't be someone that I know.

"I am quite well, sir, but thank you for asking," she said, aware of how stupid she sounded even as the words left her mouth. "If you continue on your way I am sure that I will be fine."

"Thing is, you're lying on the pavement," said the kneeling man. "Not at all the thing to leave a damsel lying in the street. What would my mother say?"

"Since there is no likelihood of your mother finding out about this incident, Perry, I doubt she will say anything about it at all," drawled his companion.

"Perhaps so, but still not going to leave the poor girl sprawled on the pavement, now am I? Bad Ton, you see. Devilish bad Ton." He turned back to Bella and stretched his hand out to her for a second time. "Allow me to help you to your feet, my dear girl. Catch a cold sitting on the pavement like that. Find you a chair if you need to sit. Better than the floor, you see."

Feeling her cheeks grow hot with embarrassment, Bella took Mr Perry's hand with considerable reluctance.

"Thank you, I am sorry to be of inconvenience to you both. I wish both of you gentlemen goodnight and thank you for your help."

She clambered to her feet, managing to keep her face covered with the hood. It restricted her ability to see her would-be rescuers, but at least it meant they had no chance to clearly see her face, either.

Mr Perry seemed to be offended by her speech. "My dear girl, what sort of ramshackle fellows do you think we are? Leaving a young lady to make her own way home at this hour? Unheard of!"

Bella was alarmed by his reaction. "Oh dear, I am sorry Mr Perry, I did not mean-" but her stumbling apology was cut short by the sarcastic laughter of Perry's tall companion.

"I suspect that your terminology in inaccurate, my friend. I highly doubt that a lady of quality would be walking unattended through Mayfair at two o'clock in the morning, don't you? I suspect she is more a ladybird than a lady."

"How dare you?" gasped Bella, curling her hands into fists. "What right do you have to insult me in such a way? I have a perfectly valid reason for being here unattended, and it is quite uncivil, rude and... and bad Ton for you to suggest otherwise!"

"Oh, I never doubted that your reasons were valid, my dear girl, but that does not make them virtuous, now does it?"

"You are the most horrible man I have ever had the misfortune to meet!" snapped Bella, but her angry response only served to make him laugh. Her cheeks burned with embarrassment, and although she could understand his reaction, she had no wish to forgive him for it.

"Now there's no need to be like that! Calm down, the both of you!" spluttered Mr Perry.

He made a strange fluttering gesture at his companion, as though he was trying to swat a fly only he could see, before turning back to Bella with an elegant bow.

"Beg your pardon – my friend is not normally so rude! Of course, you have every reason to be here, never doubted your word for a moment!"

The tall man gave a snort of contempt. Bella

chose to ignore him instead of rising to the bait, however much she longed to box his ears.

"I should hope not, Mr Perry," she said with a little sniff. "There is never any call to be ill-mannered."

"Very true, but he's a trifle bosky so there's no need to pay any attention to him," he replied with a loud whisper. "Now, tell me your direction, and I will see you safely to the door."

Hope flared in Bella's heart as she realised a way of completing her mission had presented itself in the unlikely guise of the dandified gentleman before her. "Thank you so much for your kindness Mr Perry, if you would be so kind as to escort me to Lord Coulbourne's townhouse, I would be most grateful for your company."

There was a moment of silence. Mr Perry stepped away from her as though she had grown a second head.

"Are you quite sure that you mean the Earl's lodgings?" he asked in a slightly bewildered tone.

Bella knew she had erred somehow, but the recollection of the importance of her errand steeled her nerves. "I am quite sure. Now, please escort me there at once."

The man called Perry didn't move; instead, he turned his gaze towards his companion with a slightly wild look in his eyes. A sense of dread filled Bella as she turned her attention back to the rude man. He had crossed his arms over his chest and was staring at her, his expression hard.

"You are Lord Colbourne," she said in a faint voice.

"You have the advantage of me," replied the Earl with cold civility, "for I do not appear to know you. My memory, however, is a lamentable thing. Perhaps I have wronged you in some way, madam, and you are here to remind me of my debt to you?"

His insinuation appalled her, and her cheeks flamed with embarrassment once again. The Earl stepped forwards to close the gap between them, and she backed away instinctively, but there was no escaping him. Lord Colbourne reached out and, with a deft flick of his wrist, pulled back the hood of her opera cloak.

"Good Lord, it's Miss Snowley!" said Mr Perry. Bella turned to look at him, then let out a gasp of surprise. Although she had only met him a handful of times at private balls, there was no mistaking the appearance of one of the most celebrated dandies in all of London.

"Mr Percival! Whatever must you think? Oh dear, I... that is, this is not how it appears, I mean-"

"I hate to interrupt this reunion," drawled Lord Colbourne as he removed his snuff-box from his jacket, "but I would much prefer it if you enlightened me as to who Miss Snowley is, Perry."

Mr Percival looked harassed. "Devil of a mess, if I do say so, an absolute devil of a mess. This is Snowley's sister Isabella, old boy."

"You say that name as though it should mean something to me."

Mr Percival made another wild gesture with his hands. "Snowley, man, Snowley! Good God, Snowley is the boy that you are duelling in the morning!"

Lord Colbourne snapped shut the lid of his snuff-box. He contemplated Bella in silence, the expression in his eyes making her feel as though he were a wolf contemplating his next meal. She shivered.

"Is she indeed? Well, perhaps we should escort Miss Snowley to my lodgings after all."

Purchase your copy of His Darling Belle today to find out what happens next in Bella's story!